LAST GAMBLE

An utterly gripping page-turner

FAITH MARTIN

writing as

MAXINE BARRY

Revised edition 2022
Joffe Books, London
www.joffebooks.com

First published in Great Britain in 2012

This paperback edition was first published
in Great Britain in 2022

Cover art by Dee Dee Book Covers

ISBN: 978-1-80405-396-6

CHAPTER ONE

Charmaine Reece looked at the vision in the mirror and laughed. That was *not* her! Definitely not.

And yet it was.

Large blue eyes, the exact colour of Ceylon sapphires, gazed back at her, the lashes flattered and elongated by unfamiliar mascara. Arched, delicate brows were likewise darkened and framed what others had always assured her were her most bewitching feature. Not that she'd ever believed them.

She shook her head, watching with bemused wonderment as her newly cut, water-straight hair shimmered gloriously, falling well past her shoulders. Almost silver in colour, it now had glints of old gold, courtesy of the company's hair stylist.

A pale plum lipstick complemented the figure-hugging deep plum sarong dress she was wearing, and long, long legs tapered to trim ankles and a flattering, strappy pair of white sandals. She wore no jewellery.

She felt almost naked, uncomfortably aware that she was braless beneath the wrap-around silky material, and that she wore only the skimpiest of bikini briefs.

She felt like a fraud. A ridiculous fraud.

Taking a deep breath, she walked to the door, locking her hotel room behind her and heading for the reception area and then on out into the blazing Bahamian sunshine.

In front of her, the small hotel garden gave way to the breathtaking panorama that was Gold Rock Beach.

It hadn't been hard to persuade Jo-Jo to come here for a photoshoot, especially with the discount the hotel had been willing to cut them when they discovered the amount of glamour and cachet that Jonniee, one of Britain's leading fashion houses, would be bringing with them.

Not that the girls had felt particularly glamorous after the long night flight. But Charmaine, at least, was too tense to flop into bed and grapple with jetlag. Now that she was here, she was eager to check out the lair of her enemy.

But to do that, she needed to look her best. She needed to look every inch the successful model. Just in case. Even though her chances of running into Payne Lacey right away were almost zero.

Although she had no doubt that, even at this hour, the fabulous and renowned Palace Casino next door would be open, she doubted if the manager-owner himself put in a personal appearance much before midnight. If then.

Still, it never hurt to be prepared. And she had to get used to looking and dressing like a million dollars, even if, in her heart, she felt strictly bargain basement!

She was sure that, sooner or later, one of the other girls, one of the real models, was going to catch on to the fact that she was a fraud. Only Jo-Jo knew the truth. Or at least, some of it.

For Jo-Jo, her flamboyant business partner, this was all a bit of a laugh. Like everyone else in her life, he thought she needed to live a little, break out of her rut, and throw her usual innate caution to the wind and experience life to the full. So when she'd suggested doing some modelling herself on one of their fashion shoots, he'd been only to eager to encourage her.

But she knew he wouldn't be feeling quite so relaxed if he knew why she'd really persuaded him to come here. Why she really wanted to be at Gold Rock Beach, right next to the famous 'Palace', and dressed like this.

And, with a bit of luck, he would never need to know. She'd have brought Payne Lacey to his knees, broken his heart, and be back on her way home to England before the photos had even had a chance to be developed.

She walked onto the pavement, sternly ignoring the siren call of the white sandy beach and the bright azure of the Caribbean Sea and turned instead to walk the short distance to the entrance of the Palace.

And, reputedly, that's exactly what it looked like on the inside. She bit her lip, then remembered her perfectly applied lipstick just in time. She wasn't used to wearing make-up. Nor a thousand pounds' worth of designer couture either, if it came to it. Even if she *had* designed it herself.

As she walked through the intricately wrought-iron gates into the lush, tropical paradise that was the casino's grounds, she felt suddenly cold. In spite of the bird song, the primordial sound of the sea and the scent of exotic blooms, she shivered. Somewhere, close by, he was here.

Skirting the lush roses, bird-of-paradise flowers, oleander and hibiscus bushes, she stared grimly at the edifice in front of her.

Here people came from all over the globe to answer the lure of the blackjack table, to sing the song of the roulette wheel, and revel in the excitement of the cards.

The Palace was built like something from Versailles, its shimmering stone imported, she supposed, from some far-off place. Grey-slated turrets and sloping roofs gave way to wide windows, graced with wrought-iron balconies. Bougainvillaea climbed the white-painted walls, almost hurting the eyes with the brilliance of their colour. Inside, she knew, would be marble, gold plate, silver, chandeliers, plush carpeting, all creating an illusion of grandeur to make the pulse race.

And all as fake and as worthless as the man who owned it.

Didn't those millionaires who came here to lose their money so carelessly realise that they were just lining the pockets of a charlatan? A man with a till where his heart should be, and a money-making machine in place of a human brain?

And what of those normal, everyday people, hard-working tourists out for a little taste of the high life. Just a little taste. Surely no harm in that? Lose a few chips here, drop some foreign-looking coins in a slot machine there. Didn't they realise that they were just throwing their hard-earned money away on a man who'd already gambled and won millions?

Charmaine realised her hands were clenched into hard fists, her knuckles white with tell-tale fury, and forced herself to take deep breaths. She must be calm.

She was so close now. All the hard work and planning had been done. She'd positioned herself, in an advantageous light, to within a hair's breadth of the enemy. Everything was set and ready.

She moved closer, fascinated by the size and lure of the Palace. A doorman, dressed in livery, came down the wide, fan-shaped steps as a Rolls-Royce Silver Ghost pulled up in front. A man in flowing Arabian robes stepped outside, and nodded gracefully as the doorman held open one of a double pair of heavily decorated doors that had come from a ruined monastery somewhere in Tuscany.

Since acquiring the Palace, legend had it that Payne Lacey had spared no expense in making sure that it lived up to its name.

It was known that several suites on the second and third floors were leased to the fabulously wealthy, famous and reclusive for exorbitant rates. One rumour that had since passed into legend had it that a star of Hollywood's silver screen from the fifties, mysteriously retired and never seen for over thirty years, lived in the penthouse.

Looking at the casino, Charmaine could believe it. She felt as if she'd stepped into a Gothic novel. And that somewhere inside, like an evil Mr Rochester, Payne Lacey was aware of her presence. He knew why she'd come, and was laughing at her, waiting for her to make her move. Confident of defeating and humiliating her before she could even so much as say her first word. Which was nonsense, of course. But still, just the thought of it was enough to make her blood run cold.

She shook her head, then jumped as a noise to her left made her swivel around, blue eyes wide in alarm.

But it was only a gardener.

She felt like laughing, except that it wasn't really funny. If just the mere thought of Payne Lacey could sap her confidence like this, making her react like a silly pre-school child hearing her first scary fairy story, then what realistic chance did she have of getting her revenge?

She moved forward, intrigued by the skill of fast-flying shears. He was squatting down with his broad back turned towards her, and as she watched, the sunlight rippled over his muscles, highlighting the ridges of shoulders and the lean expanse of smooth, bronze skin. He was wearing cut-off jeans, the denim almost white with age and wear, the ends ragged and looking like little white feathers against his powerful thighs.

He seemed oblivious to her presence, and as he duck-walked to the next area of overgrown greenery, she saw the tendons in his thighs stand out.

He was in superb shape, and she could understand why. Such huge gardens would require constant care and hard physical labour. And in this heat, too. Used to the cooler northern climes of her native Oxfordshire, Charmaine could feel her own strength wilting in the strong Caribbean sunshine.

This man, though, looked set to continue clipping and weeding, mowing and pruning for hours. Small rivulets of sweat beaded the hard planes of his cheeks, running to drip off his chin, glinting with the remains of a golden stubble.

He turned his head sharply, suddenly aware of her, and the cool grey eyes, as deep as a stormy ocean, took her by surprise.

His hair was dark gold, the colour of newly harvested corn, and she'd expected eyes the colour of her own. Not eyes like steel. They regarded her boldly, moving from her shining silvery hair to the tips of her toes.

'Hello,' she said, trying to shake off her discomfort under his gaze. She really was going to have to develop a much tougher skin than this if she was to survive the ordeal of the next few days. 'That looks like hard work.' Although naturally friendly by nature, she had always been plagued by shyness. Something, of course, a top-flight fashion model would never be!

The gardener turned and slowly stood up. And up. And up.

Charmaine blinked nervously and took an involuntary step back. Although, at five feet eight, she wasn't exactly short herself, he seemed to tower over her. As he turned, she couldn't help but notice that the muscles on his biceps matched those of his powerful thighs. His stomach was tight and washboard hard, his chest hairless and even more deeply bronzed than his back. In contrast, his light hair and grey eyes seemed even more disconcerting.

'Plants deserve hard work,' he said simply, his accent throwing her. It sounded American, and yet had a lilting, almost musical undertone that she knew she recognised, and yet couldn't quite place.

It was an odd thing to say, and she wasn't quite sure how to respond. His eyes moved over the silken flow of the sarong dress — the way it hugged her full breasts, clung to her waist like a lover, then wrapped sensuously around her thighs. His lips began to twist into a smile. A speculative look rose to his eyes.

Her skin began to tingle, as if someone was rubbing ice-cold sorbet all over it. She took a deep breath and told herself to relax. The other models would have taken a look like that in their stride.

They certainly wouldn't feel like running a mile!

'I take it you like working here,' she managed to mumble, casting a somewhat helpless look around the lush garden. She almost groaned. What a pathetic thing to say. Why didn't she have the ability to flirt, like the other girls? They'd had the male staff on the plane twisted around their fingers.

Although, in all fairness, Charmaine didn't think that this particular male of the species was all that twistable. Not even for someone like Jinx, the superstar of the upcoming Jonniee fashion shoot.

As if to confirm this instinctive understanding, the giant Adonis in front of her smiled. It was a strange smile, as if she'd said something unintentionally amusing.

'Oh, it has its compensations,' he agreed, casually tossing down the pair of shears he was carrying and pushing back a lock of sweat-darkened hair that had fallen over his brow.

He moved towards her, his long loping strides eating the short distance between them, making her retreat hastily. She flushed when he raised a sardonic brow, looked pointedly at the newly created distance between them, then merely stooped to retrieve a bottle of mineral water that had been resting near her feet.

Taking the top off, he drank deeply.

She watched, fascinated, the movement of his Adam's apple as it moved up and down the strong, tanned column of his throat. When he finished, he wiped the top of the bottle and put the top back on.

'What's the matter?' he asked softly. 'Did you think I was going to grab you and ravish you in the bushes?'

Charmaine, for one mad moment, had thought something exactly like that. Although why she should assume a man like this would be interested in her, she couldn't have said. A man who looked as good as this, living and working on a tourist island that was annually inundated with gorgeous female holidaymakers, must have his pick of beautiful women.

She laughed nervously, and its utter falseness made her wince deep inside.

'No. No, of course not,' she denied.

But even as she spoke, she was aware that this Adonis of a man, this gorgeous blond giant, knew that she was lying.

He looked at her, a slightly puzzled expression pulling his dark brows together.

'You *are* one of the models doing a shoot over here, aren't you?' he said, making her stiffen in sudden alarm.

'Yes. How did you know?' she asked, far more sharply than she'd meant to.

The stranger grinned sardonically. 'Did you think it was a big secret or something? The whole island — well, this part of it anyway — knows that some models from England are doing a fashion shoot on the beach here and up at the casino.'

'Oh,' she said, feeling somewhat deflated. Yes, that made sense. Certainly Payne Lacey would have been at pains to make sure that everybody knew about it. For wasn't it just one more feather in his cap? Owning a place coveted by a top-ranking fashion house?

'For a fashion model you sure are jumpy,' the gardener said, distracting her dark thoughts and replacing them once again with fear.

Was she so obviously a phoney? So much of a fraud that even a humble gardener could spot her weakness?

'What do you mean?' she said, trying to inject some scorn into her voice, some world-weary cynicism.

Those arctic ocean eyes swept over her again, and a dismissive grin made her blood begin to simmer. 'Forget it,' he said casually, reaching down once more for the shears.

'No,' she insisted. 'I mean it. What did you mean by that crack? I'm not jumpy.' Not much!

He glanced back across at her from his contemplation of the hedge. 'No? Then why are you acting like a virgin who's just wandered by mistake into an orgy?'

Charmaine blinked. 'Wh-what did you just say?' she stuttered. She couldn't have heard him right.

Could she?

'You see,' he said, grinning again, shaking his head as if she was providing him with no end of entertainment. 'You looked shocked to the core. And here I was, thinking all fashion models were hard-as-nails, seen-it-all, done-it-all women of the world.'

Charmaine felt her cheeks flame, and groaned inwardly. Oh no. Not now. Why did she have to be so cursed with shyness? All her life, she'd battled an almost paralysing bashfulness.

And besides, he was right. She *was* worlds away from the other models currently sleeping off jetlag back at the hotel. From their conversation on the flight over, she knew that most of them were exactly as this aggravating blond giant had described. Strong, sophisticated, sexually confident young women. A world away from herself. She'd never even taken a lover yet. And everybody knew that twenty-four was ridiculously old to still be a virgin.

How was she ever going to convince someone like Payne Lacey that she belonged in his world of gambling, champagne, high living and sexual conquest if she couldn't even fool a gardener?

The blond stranger watched, fascinated, as her colour ebbed and flowed. Her remarkable blue eyes darkened, became shadows. He watched her exquisite shoulders actually begin to droop.

When he'd first turned and seen her, he'd been stunned. Literally. He'd felt like the proverbial mullet, zapped with a lightning bolt. But not for the world would he have shown it. Faking more interest in the rare shrub he was pruning than her own far more beautiful self had simply given him the means to get himself under control.

It hadn't taken him two seconds to figure out she must be one of the models from England. Nobody but a fashion model for a firm as prestigious as Jonniee could look half so gorgeous. That elegant sarong dress, that silver hair, those eyes set in such a perfect face.

And that sort of trouble he could do without.

Now, though, as he watched her blush, he wondered just what in the hell was going on. Since when did women as beautiful as this one, with the world at their feet, act like a Victorian maiden being propositioned by a rascally footman?

'This is my first shoot,' he heard her say, somewhat forlornly, and glanced at her sharply. Was she kidding? No, he realised, a moment later, she wasn't. As incredible as it seemed, she looked unsure of herself. Ah. So that explained it. She was just a baby piranha in the making and not a fully-fledged member of the shark club yet.

He felt himself smiling cynically. But once she saw herself on the front cover of *Vogue*, once playboys driving Ferraris fell over themselves to take her out to dine in Paris, and men fought to buy her the biggest diamonds, then things would be different.

'Don't worry, you'll ace it,' he said starkly, and although the words should have comforted her, somehow they didn't.

Hopelessly confused, she merely smiled uncertainly. 'I hope so.' A lot depended on it. And besides, she owed it to Jo-Jo not to entirely mess up his shoot.

'I hear it's really nice inside there. Mr Lacey's supposed to have spent millions on it,' she said instead, steering the conversation to where she needed it to go. Not that she expected a mere gardener to be able to tell her much. Why, Charmaine thought, indignant on his behalf, she'd bet her year's salary that this man had never even seen inside it.

'So they say,' he confirmed wryly, fascinated by the play of emotions that crossed her face.

Just then, a man turned down the path towards them. Dressed in a white linen tropical suit, a natty Panama hat and casual Gucci loafers, he looked a typical Palace candidate.

'Charmaine! Hey, there you are. I thought I saw you wandering down this way.'

Charmaine smiled brightly at Jo-Jo as he wound his way across to her, and she smiled even more widely as his dark brown eyes widened at the sight of the Adonis.

She could see his interest quicken.

'Hello. This is my part— er, the owner of Jonniee,' Charmaine said, stumbling over her near mistake. For although, to the world in general, Jo-Jo was Jonniee, only those in the business were aware that Charmaine Reece was the creative and designing force behind the fashion house. Jo-Jo, although occasionally coming up with the odd stunning creation, was much more the 'front man'. He did the television appearances and the magazine interviews. He was more than happy to play the fashion guru and reel in the big buyers.

And although he'd often nagged Charmaine to be far more than his near-silent partner, she seemed to like living in the shadows. The limelight had never been for her.

The gardener's eyes narrowed on hearing her slip. He glanced at Jo-Jo with weary eyes. Saw a thirty-something, good-looking man, who could boost an up-and-coming model's career into the stratosphere.

The smile he gave Charmaine was of grim irony. So much for the maidenly blushes. Or maybe she was just an old-fashioned girl after all? When all was said and done, sleeping with the boss to get on was an old and trusted tradition.

Charmaine had no trouble reading his thoughts, and felt herself go cold all over. She lifted her chin, hoping for a proud and haughty look, but inside she felt herself shrivelling up. This man thought she was cheap.

But what did it matter? He was nothing. Meant nothing. She'd probably never even see him again.

'Well, we'll leave you to get on,' she said, but her voice merely sounded hurt. Not at all haughty and proud.

'Jo-Jo, let's have some champagne,' she said brightly, watching as her business partner's eyes widened in surprise. He knew as well as she that she didn't drink. But, bless him, he didn't let her down.

'Sure, sweetheart, just what I was thinking. The sun doesn't have to be over the yardarm for *me* to break out the Bolly.'

She took his arm and let him lead her away, but all the time she could feel the glare of glacial grey eyes boring into her back.

And she felt, absurdly, like crying.

CHAPTER TWO

Darkness fell suddenly that night, and from her tiny hotel balcony, Charmaine watched, enchanted, as the sun set over the sea, turning the evening from shimmering red to violet, to deepest purple.

The ringing of the telephone shattered the quiet, and reluctantly tearing her eyes away from the first twinkling stars appearing in the warm tropical night sky, she picked up the receiver, smiling instantly as she recognised her sister's voice.

'Hi, sis, how's paradise?'

Charmaine laughed and sat down on the edge of the bed. 'Fine, just lovely. How's Desdemona shaping up?'

'Oh, you know. Same as ever. Someday I'm going to find a director who actually wants her to fight back!'

Lucy, her half-sister, was currently wowing Stratford-upon-Avon critics with her portrayal of Shakespeare's tragic heroine.

'But you're getting standing ovations. Mother would have been so proud,' she pointed out.

Their mother had been an actress too, appearing in many British films in the fifties and sixties, before dying ten years ago. Her second marriage to Charmaine's father had failed, although both girls were still very close to him. A well-respected actor himself, he had always been disappointed with Charmaine's lack of talent, and had always regarded her success in the fashion world as a poor second best. Not that he'd ever said so. But both girls knew that Lucy, although not his blood, was far more his daughter.

'I know. I'm thinking of trying to break into films. I've had it with this starving-artist-in-a-garret gig. My agent thinks it's a good time for it. So who knows? My next call might be from Hollywood.'

Charmaine laughed. She could almost picture Lucy's face, gamin, mobile, a perfect blank canvas for any emotion she cared to portray. But her voice, when it came next, sounded pensive, and Charmaine felt her knuckles tighten on the receiver.

'So, you're on Grand Bahama,' she said, her voice too carefully nonchalant to be sincere. 'I somehow assumed you'd be in the capital.'

'Oh, you know Jo-Jo,' Charmaine said, hoping her voice didn't sound as tense as she felt. 'He had his heart set on a specific beach.' She didn't mention the casino. She knew she must never mention that. If Lucy got just one whiff of what she was up to . . .

'How are you feeling? No stage fright?' she asked, trying to change the subject.

'Nope,' Lucy reassured her. 'I'm having too much fun playing the fair Desdemona to be suffering from stage fright. Besides, Othello is quite a dish. We're going out for Thai food tonight at this new restaurant by the river.' Charmaine was pleased. It was only dinner with a fellow actor, but nonetheless a promising sign that her sister's heart was healing.

For the next five minutes the two sisters chatted happily, then, with a little cry at the sight of the time, Charmaine said she had to go, and they rang off, promising to speak tomorrow.

She showered quickly, washing and blow-drying her hair, before tying it back in a complicated but flattering French pleat.

Next, she walked to her wardrobe and drew out the dark brown velvet dress. Too warm, really, for a balmy Bahamian night, but she needed it to boost her confidence. It was one of her own creations, from autumn of last year. Cut with almost puritanical simplicity, it clung to her like poured chocolate. A deep v, narrow but plunging almost to her navel at the front, was repeated with a wider v at the back, bearing the delicate bones and contours of her shoulders and spine. It clung tightly to thighs and hips, and stopped just above the ankle. Accessorising this with a matching pair of chocolate brown high-heels, she completed the ensemble with long amber and tiger's-eye earrings and a delicate tiger's-eye pendant that nestled in her cleavage.

As she suspected, the contrast to her lightly sun-kissed skin and bright fair hair was stunning.

She kept the make-up to a minimum. Rebecca, one of Jonniee's make-up girls, had always assured her that she had perfect skin, and since Charmaine was still too much a novice with more complicated make-up, she decided to keep it simple. A little blusher, a touch of mascara and darkening to the brows, and a neutral lipstick.

She looked perfect for what she needed to do tonight. She looked like a model.

Gone was the girl who felt happiest in jeans and T-shirts, creating gorgeous evening gowns for others in the converted attic/studio of her small cottage. Gone was the girl who'd disappointed her father with her inability to even so much as star in the school nativity play. Gone was the shy, retiring girl who boys quickly gathered around, only to quickly leave again when they realised what a lie her looks truly were.

Because she didn't know how to flirt. Didn't know how to give them what they wanted. A pang for all those remembered and lonely nights shot through her, but she quickly shut them away. Time to concentrate on business. It was the illusion that mattered, after all. Her enemy would not see through the disguise, of that she was confident.

Tonight, the entire Jonniee gang was going to the Palace. It had been Jo-Jo's idea, to give them an advance feel for the place. So tonight was the night — she could just feel it in her bones — when she'd be coming face to face with Payne Lacey.

The man who had almost killed her sister.

* * *

Payne Lacey checked the slim gold Patek Philippe watch on his wrist, and nodded. Not yet midnight and already the place was packed.

He was wearing black, not a tuxedo, but tailored slacks and jacket that had Savile Row written all over them. A white silk shirt with two buttons opened at the neck. Black Italian loafers, designed just for him by a little cobbler he'd discovered in Napoli, looked right at home against the plush navy-blue and gold-flecked Aubusson carpet that adorned the main salon.

Genuine oils lined oak-panelled rooms. Blazing chandeliers cast bright, sparkling light over the baize tables. At one of the corner tables, a Japanese billionaire was losing at poker, being fleeced by a delighted, unable-to-believe-his luck rancher from Wyoming.

The song of the slot machines from the hall contrasted with the murmur of voices and the clink of Baccarat crystal glassware as waiters and waitresses circled with champagne and their speciality cocktail. There were no clocks. The musical entertainment was confined to the next room. Nothing to distract the concentration of card players, dice throwers and roulette watchers.

He turned, amused and curious, as Jean-Luc, the head waiter, hurried forward towards the entrance to the main gambling salon, his normally unimpressed features creasing into a smile of welcome.

And a moment later he saw why. The fashion-house contingent had arrived.

A redhead in green led the way into the room, but just as her eyes lasered onto his, a vision in silver-gold and dark chocolate appeared behind her. In contrast to the see-through gauzy material the redhead was wearing, the dark depth of velvet the other woman wore transfixed him. Payne could feel his hands tingle, as if they were already caressing her. Unlike velvet, her skin, he knew, would be silky and warm and pulsing with life to his touch.

She turned to speak to the man behind her, and he saw with naked approval the elegant turn of her shoulders, the silken rope of hair that bounced almost to the level of her delightfully rounded derrière.

Again he felt the urge to go across to her, to run his finger down the length of her spine, to cup her buttocks in his hands, to trace the line of her hips. He walked swiftly towards her.

The blonde vision turned, saw him, and froze.

He smiled as a look of utter consternation crossed her lovely face.

'Hello, I'm Payne Lacey. Welcome to the Palace,' he said, vaguely aware that the redhead had pounced on him, looping one hand over his arm and was laughing huskily up at him.

'Thanks. I'm Jinx,' she purred.

'Of course you are,' he replied, hiding his impatience with her behind a bland smile, before turning to the male of the group.

'And you must be Gareth John Jones. Payne Lacey.' He held out a hand firmly.

'Oh, call me Jo-Jo,' he said at once, taking the outstretched hand with pleasure. 'And I can see you've already met Jinx,' he said dryly. 'Try to ignore her — she's a strumpet. This is . . .'

The rest of the introductions washed over Payne, however, as his gaze refused to leave the wide blue eyes that began to cool and then spit sapphire fire at him.

Charmaine felt dizzy. She even wondered, for one insane moment, if she was dreaming — having a nightmare — so unreal did the moment seem. This couldn't be true. It couldn't be real. She had rehearsed this in her mind over and over again, the moment when she finally came face to face with her enemy.

She knew he'd be good-looking, charming and sophisticated. Lucy never fell for any other kind of man. And she'd expected to see him look at her speculatively, perhaps wondering arrogantly how long it would take him to bed her. She'd planned on smiling aloofly, telling him without words that he'd never do it. She'd imagined his confidence begin to waver, to see just a flicker of interest quicken in his jaded eyes as he recognised a challenge.

And after that, she would play it by ear.

But this was nothing like she imagined. How could this man be Payne Lacey?

There'd been a mistake. There had to be. Or someone was playing a practical joke on her.

'But you're the gardener,' she whispered helplessly.

Jinx laughed. 'Hardly the gardener,' she purred, running a hand across Payne's sleeve. He was by far the best looking man here. And the owner of the casino too! A brief holiday affair would be just the thing.

'No, she's right. Come on, 'fess up,' Jo-Jo said, sensing Charmaine's shock. He too had been somewhat surprised to find the tanned, nearly butt-naked Adonis of the afternoon meeting them this evening as the suave host. 'Just what were you doing pruning the hedges?'

Jinx's green eyes sharpened. What was this?

'It wasn't a hedge but a hybrid. My head gardener and I have been breeding for some time,' Payne corrected him. 'Not many people know about my passion for botany though. And it would almost certainly ruin my reputation as a lazy dilettante if it got out, so I'll ask you to keep quiet about it,' he said dryly.

'Well, well, a Renaissance man,' Jinx purred. 'Who'd have thought it.'

Who indeed, Charmaine thought grimly. Her anger, slow to build, began to boil. That he shared her passion for gardens only made her feel even more wrong-footed.

17

He'd known all along that she'd mistaken him for a hired hand. How he must have been laughing at her behind her back all this time. Even when she'd asked him about the inside of the casino, he'd pretended not to know or care.

Payne watched her anger build, and a tense excitement began to roil in the pit of his stomach. Her cheekbones flushed with temper, and she began to tremble, like the warning breeze that foreshadowed a hurricane. He felt himself holding his breath, waiting for the magnificent storm of scorn to break through.

But she swallowed it all back.

He saw her doing it, saw her struggling with her inner self, and felt bitterly disappointed. He'd been looking forward to crossing swords with her.

Instead, she smiled feebly. Why?

Then he realised that, of course, she couldn't afford to make a bad impression on her boss and lover. Sleeping with Jo-Jo might have got her onto the shoot and off to a flying start in the supermodel stakes, but insulting the owner of the casino where he hoped to shoot would hardly make for good bedtime conversation later on that night.

Payne smiled wolfishly, knowing he had her right where he wanted her. And at the same time, tried to pretend that the thought of her belonging to another man didn't make him feel like chewing the expensive, hand-painted wallpaper right off the walls.

'Let's dance, gambling man,' Jinx purred, pulling on his arm coquettishly, and he sighed slightly. But there was nothing else a gentleman could do but oblige the lady.

'Of course, I'd be delighted,' he said smoothly, steering her through the main salon to a small bar, dance and stage area. It was mostly empty, for although a sultry nightclub singer, justly famous on the islands, sang the blues to the accompaniment of a visiting New Orleans jazz combo, few came to the Palace to drink or dance.

Jinx nestled into him sensuously, but he was already looking over her shoulder, watching as some of the other models, the chief photographer, Charmaine and Jo-Jo wandered around the salons, checking out possible photo opportunities, before heading up to the bar.

When the song ended, he firmly led Jinx to the others, and deposited her on a bar stool, ordering her a choice of drink, on the house.

Then he turned to Charmaine, her cameo profile perfect in the soft lighting. Behind him, the throaty-voiced singer began to sing 'I Only Have Eyes For You'.

His lips twisted in self-mockery. How appropriate.

'You don't mind if I steal your lady from you for a dance, do you, Mr Jones?' he asked, holding out his hand to Charmaine, who stared at it like a rabbit might stare at a hooded cobra.

'Jo-Jo, please,' he responded, eyeing first the casino owner then his friend, an arch, speculative look creeping across his face.

'Oh, she's not his,' Jinx drawled spitefully, not best pleased at being dismissed so quickly.

Charmaine, having no other choice, reluctantly put her hand in his, but her legs shook as he led her to the dance floor. The neon-blue lighting and lingering smoke from the scented table candles reminded her of the kind of films where Bette Davis planned seduction and murder, and in which men were men, and women knew it! And she had to fight back the absurd desire to laugh. She was utterly out of her depth here. She must have been out of her mind to think she could ever pull this off.

'Relax,' the deep timbre of his voice, with that underlying melodic resonance that so thrilled her, whispered across the top of her head, his breath rustling the tendrils of hair on her forehead. He was so close, if he just bent his head a few more millimetres, his lips would be brushing her brow.

She shuddered as she longed, suddenly and violently, for him to do just that. To trail his lips across her temple, down beside her eye, to move across to kiss the tip of her nose and down to her mouth.

She firmed her lips against the imagined touch, but they throbbed, as if feeling cheated.

19

His arm felt like a band of molten steel around her waist, his fingers, resting on the bare skin of her back, like branding irons. Her thighs, encased in the velvet of her dress, trembled against the length of his own, and she was sure he must be able to feel it.

Her head swam as she fought to get her breathing under control. She couldn't faint now. Couldn't do something so ignominious. And yet, she felt as if she was floating.

She didn't know what was happening in the world outside. Here, on the dance floor, there was only the two of them. Payne's voice, his breath on her hair, his arms around her, the length of her body pressed to his. She was breathing in his scent, her very heartbeat synchronising itself to his.

'You're beautiful,' he said softly. 'But then, you must hear that every day. From lots of men.'

Charmaine's eyes snapped open. The spell abruptly broke.

She wondered, with something approaching hysteria, what he would say if she told him that, no, men in fact never said that to her. She never gave them the chance. On the rare occasions that she had dated, she never followed up on that first meal out, or that first visit to the cinema.

It was Lucy who was the famous actress. Lucy who could be really beautiful, just because she made people believe that she was so. Lucy who had the charm, the talent, the appeal. It had always been so.

Charmaine just designed dresses.

For a moment, she felt an intense longing to be back home. Safe in her cottage, with her cat, Wordsworth, and the garden that she loved to fill with all the old-fashioned country garden plants. There all was calm and right with her world. Here, she was lost. Buffeted by sensations and feelings that were alien and strange. And, she was sure, dangerous.

Unspeakably dangerous.

'Your friend is well named,' he said, wondering what was making her shake all over again. Surely it wasn't her temper coming back.

'Who? Jo-Jo?'

'No. Jinx.'

And suddenly Charmaine was burbling with laughter. He hadn't fallen for the super-glamorous model after all, then. When she'd seen them dancing, with Jinx's flame-red hair against his shoulder, they'd looked so right together. But they'd only danced the once, and she'd hoped, oh how she'd hoped, that she hadn't imagined it when he'd seemed relieved to deposit her back at the bar.

Now she knew she'd been right.

'Most men fall for Jinx like a ton of bricks,' she felt obliged to point out.

'And isn't she just used to it,' he drawled. 'No. I'm much more interested in you.'

Charmaine stumbled against him.

'You are?' she whispered. Her heart seemed to lift, then plunge, like a bird about to take wing, then realising, just before it was too late, that it couldn't actually fly.

'Mmm-hmm,' he confirmed lazily. 'Just what makes you tick, Charmaine? One moment you're the hard-bitten woman with her eye on the main chance. The next, you're all a-tremble.'

Charmaine pulled her head back to look at him. 'What do you mean? What main chance?'

'Oh come on,' Payne said. 'Don't tell me you're not sleeping with the boss?'

Charmaine gasped. She stepped back, her eyes firing up like an acetylene torch. Payne felt a huge surge of desire hit him. Yes. Now. Now she would erupt.

'You certainly live up to your name, don't you?' Charmaine hissed. 'Payne by name, and pain by nature.'

'Whereas you don't,' he shot back. 'You may be Charmaine by name, but charming by nature — I don't think so.'

He laughed then winced as she kicked him on the shin.

His jaw tightened, but his dancing step never faltered. In fact, Charmaine realised, they were still dancing, and had never stopped.

'For your information,' she hissed, 'Jo-Jo is gay. He's been living with his partner, Peter, a top investment banker, for nearly ten years now.'

Payne smiled. 'Is that a fact,' he said smugly.

And Charmaine realised how neatly he'd tricked her into divulging information. Information she could have used to her advantage, if only she'd kept her big mouth shut. She could have used Jo-Jo to make him jealous. Or even to act as a much-needed shield and buffer.

Too late now.

Her eyes narrowed. She drew her foot back in preparation.

'Ah, ah, ah,' he said warningly, turning sharply, pivoting her around and bending her supple back over his arm, laughingly neutralising her. 'No more kicking.'

Charmaine clung on to his shoulders, despair burning deep inside her.

It was all going wrong again!

First the disastrous start, now this. If she was going to go through with her plan, she had to pull her socks up! How was she ever going to win him over when she kicked his shins like a frustrated schoolgirl?

But she knew only too well what had come over her. Temper. And fear. For the first time in her sheltered, ordered, calm life, she was out of control.

And she didn't like it.

Didn't she? A small voice whispered like a genie from the depths of a bottle. Wasn't it heady? Wasn't it wonderful? To have a man like this one interested in her? Wasn't it just blissful? The voice seemed to come at her from all directions at once — her mind, her heart, the place where her dreams lived.

As he pulled her closer to him, as she felt his hand slip down to rest suggestively against her buttocks and she felt her insides become fluid with molten heat, she began to wonder.

Her head rested almost wearily against his shoulder. It was no good fighting it. It felt gloriously right to be here. To be held like this, by this man, dancing as closely in his arms as the laws of physics would allow, giddy with excitement and recklessness.

'That's more like it,' Payne said softly. And smiled tenderly over her head. What a contradiction she was. She seemed so unsure of herself, and yet she was easily the most beautiful woman he'd ever seen.

And she was free and unencumbered. And she'd be on the island for the next week or so, which was the perfect length of time for a blissful, guilt-free affair.

The song came to a poignant end, and in a daze, Charmaine pulled away.

Was she mad? This was the man who'd broken her sister's heart. A man so callous he could, and did, regard women as nothing more than disposable items for his pleasure. And she'd nearly fallen into the same trap herself. But she was all right now. She was ready for him. The plan was back on track.

She looked up into eyes that were now as soft and as grey as a wood pigeon's wing.

'Dance with me again?' he said softly, confident of her answer.

Charmaine smiled coolly. 'No. I don't think so,' she said calmly, then turned and walked away from him.

He watched her in silence for a few seconds, standing utterly still, then forced a wolfish grin to his face, ignoring the tiny kernel of hurt that had for some reason wormed its way to his heart.

So she wanted to play rough.

Well, if that's the way she wanted it, he was always willing to oblige a lady.

CHAPTER THREE

The beach was idyllic — a curving crescent moon of white sand, palm trees, a calm aquamarine sea, and glorious, glorious sunlight.

As she nervously approached the Jonniee crew, set up midway on the beach, Charmaine could see that the junior photographer was already murmuring ecstatic comments about the quality of light as he gazed into his light meter. Phil, the senior photographer, was already set up, surrounded by the paraphernalia of his profession. As the 'silent' partner, Charmaine had never really watched photoshoots before. Oh, she'd been present in the audience at nearly all of Jonniee's fashion shows and launches, though she had firmly resisted all of Jo-Jo's attempts to get her up on the stage afterwards to acknowledge the plaudits of the critics and buyers alike. But she'd never before seen the nuts-and-bolts business of photoshoots. Only the glossy perfection of their results in magazines and on public billboards.

Now, she watched the other four models surreptitiously. All seemed perfectly at ease in robes, lounging on deck chairs, waiting for the call to action. Fizz, a tall, stunning woman with dark skin and bone structure to die for, even seemed to be snoozing, two pieces of cucumber covering her soulful eyes. Jinx, in contrast, was here there and everywhere, fixing her make-up in the mirrors, rooting through the outfits, generally buttering up Phil. Dee-Dee, a brunette with hair even longer than Charmaine's, was reading a book. She thought she'd heard her say on the plane over that she was studying archaeology at college. The final girl, with a pixie face and a bell-bob of orange-coloured hair stared, bored, into the sea. Coral, she thought her name was.

'Relax, you'll be fine,' Jo-Jo said, coming up alongside her and making her jump. 'We already know from the try-outs we did back in London that the camera loves you.'

It was one thing to be beautiful, Jo-Jo knew, another thing altogether to be photogenic. But the freelancer he'd hired had assured him that Charmaine had the 'it' factor to be a model, if only she'd lose the bashfulness. Which was, Jo-Jo had assured him with a wink, just what he was trying to get her to do!

But now she looked as tense as a violin string. She was watching one of the gophers set up poles in the sand, tying gaily striped bed sheets along them to make a private changing enclosure for the girls, and looking as if she wished herself a thousand miles away.

'Just remember what you've learned, and you'll be fine,' he said brightly.

Tacked onto a lamp post, near the road edge of the beach, Charmaine's nervous eye caught the word 'Palace', and curious, moved a step or two closer, then grimaced as she read it.

The sign was advertising the upcoming Weekend Extravaganza celebration of Payne Lacey's decade of ownership. Already several people were reading it, discussing the promise of a truly luxurious, no-holds-barred evening of the finest wines, gourmet titbits, celebrities and of course, gambling opportunities.

'That guy sure has got it made,' she heard one of the young men sigh wistfully, a beach attendant from a hotel further up the strip. 'All the island papers are running a spread about it. As if the place doesn't rake in dollars like there's no tomorrow anyway. And to think, the guy got the place for nothing.'

Jo-Jo rose one laconic eyebrow. 'Oh, not for nothing, surely,' he protested. 'You mean it was going cheap at the time. Property prices in a rut, or was the gambling licence in doubt?'

The beach attendant, a native Bahamian, chuckled, delighted to have come across someone who didn't know the island's worst kept secret.

'No, I mean it literally. Didn't you know? Mr Lacey won the place. In a game of poker.'

Charmaine gasped. *'He what?'*

'True, I swear.' He held up a hand. 'Yves St Germaine, the owner at the time, wanted to get his hands on a small hotel Mr Lacey owned in the States. It wasn't that he wanted the hotel, you see, but because he was part of a big conglomerate that had been buying up real estate on that bit of coast in order to construct a marina.'

Charmaine smiled dryly. No doubt Payne had got wind of what was going on and bought the hotel, just so that he could force up the price when he turned out to be the only one not selling.

'Go on,' Jo-Jo said, fascinated.

'Well, the poker game got out of hand. There was some a Middle-Eastern billionaire sitting in who kept raising the stakes, and there was far too much booze flowing, or so they say. Anyway, Mr St Germaine got reckless and bet his casino against Mr Lacey's hotel, plus every cent Mr Lacey owned.'

Charmaine paled. 'And he took the bet?' she whispered, appalled. How could a man do such a thing? To bet a hotel against a property that had much more value, that was one thing. But to bet every penny?

The Bahamian grinned, no doubt with pride and respect for a man with so much courage.

'He sure did. And won too. Mr St Germaine was sick as a dog over it later, when he sobered up, and threatened to take the issue to court, but of course he didn't. There were too many high-flying witnesses for him to back out. He never did get the hotel Stateside, either. Mr Lacey held onto it to muscle his own way in onto the board of the conglomerate building the marina. They say that he made his second fortune with that.'

Charmaine had heard enough.

What kind of man did such outrageous things? What if he'd lost? What if he'd walked away from the game with only the clothes on his back?

He'd have clawed back another fortune, of course, a little voice said reprovingly in the back of her mind. What else would a man like that do?

Ruthlessly, she shrugged the thought away. A woman would never be able to trust a man like that. Never know, from one moment to the next, what insanity he might conceive of next. It would be no good giving your heart to such a man, let alone marrying him.

Charmaine brought herself up short. Marry him? Now what had made her think of that. There was no question of giving her heart to Payne Lacey. Only in making him think she had done, and then wresting his own heart back in return. Then she could take the utmost pleasure in breaking it in half and handing it back to him. On a silver platter worthy of the owner of the Palace, naturally.

'Looks as if Phil's ready to go,' Jo-Jo said, shaking her out of her reverie, and sinking her, once again, into a blue funk of nerves.

Phil called Coral up first, getting her to pose with a piece of driftwood strategically draped with seaweed. As the orange-haired pixie stood up, Charmaine saw that she'd already changed into one of her designs, a bathing suit in near-fluorescent oranges, yellows and greens, with a diaphanous beach robe.

She watched, getting more and more nervous as Coral cavorted and smiled, pouted, threw back her head, did a little jig, and generally looked the essence of flirtatious, vibrant young womanhood.

And she knew, with a sinking feeling deep in the pit of her stomach, that when it came to her turn, the gathered crowd wouldn't give her such applause. Already her feet were beginning to feel like lead, and her limbs as graceless as those of an elephant.

* * *

Payne Lacey saw the crowd the moment he stepped onto the beach. He watched, amused, as Jinx, in a navy-blue bikini top and wrap-around skirt, flirted with the camera. There was a collective gasp as she whipped off the skirt to reveal thong bikini bottoms, revealing long, long legs and tanned, rounded buttocks.

He moved around the edge of the crowd, to where he could see Charmaine watching from the sidelines.

She looked, he realised with surprise, scared to death. She went even paler as the photographer called her name.

Charmaine, heart pounding, walked unsteadily to the spot that Phil had indicated. The wind had picked up a little, creating white horses on the sea, and he wanted to incorporate them into the shoot. He'd had enough of panoramas and palms.

'Right, go back a little, so that your feet are in the foam. No, not that far,' he yelped, as the waves threatened to splash the long, wispy beach robe she had on. In creams and yellows, it would darken and show off every spot of moisture.

'Dippy, don't you know enough not to get the merchandise wet?' Jinx drawled from her sprawled position on a deck chair. Fizz, next up, looked across, surprised. Charmaine bit her lip, knowing the other girl had a right to be taken aback at such unprofessional behaviour. Then she jumped as Phil yelled at her again not to ruin her lipstick. He called to Rebecca, who obligingly retouched it.

Even from where he stood at the back, Payne could see the painful colour come then go from her face. She stood stiffly awkward, not at all with the loose-limbed grace of the other girls.

28

'OK, let me get in close . . . yes, that's it,' Phil said, much more favourably. A thin, wiry cockney in his forties, he'd seen and done it all. He cared only about getting the perfect shot, which meant cajoling or bullying the best out of the clothes and woman wearing them.

The sea breeze lifted the long, gossamer strands of her hair in a way that no wind machine could match. That, and the stark blue sky behind her, the playful sea and the rippling of the cream beach robe against her lithe form gave him, he knew, the perfect shot. Maybe even the best of the whole shoot.

If only the girl would loosen up. He knew from Jo-Jo that this was her first professional job, but surely she wasn't a complete novice?

'OK, lean forward and no . . . not that far. Think of the shadow.'

Charmaine blinked. Shadow?

'Sunlight, girl,' Jinx's voice drawled once more from the sidelines. 'Don't want the shade of your big nose or hooked chin falling over the breasts, babe,' she called loudly, making the crowd ripple with uneasy laughter.

Charmaine blushed, looking bewildered and hurt, and automatically Phil snapped furiously. He was not sure why. He knew he'd never be able to use them. The customer wanted sexy, fun, jaunty. Not haunted and sad.

But again, he knew he'd just taken a picture in a million. The wide pained eyes, the brush of hectic colour, the immobility of a face frozen in shame and time. She'd never looked more beautiful. But who would he give the picture to? Jo-Jo wouldn't want it. It was no good to Jonniee.

Realising the girl was in trouble, he forced his voice to become kind. 'OK, Charmaine, you're doing great. Just angle the head back a little, that's it, no, not your body, just your head. Yes, good, now flick back the hair a little. Don't forget to smile.'

Out of the corner of her eye, Charmaine could see Coral exchange a look with Fizz, and she fought back a groan. She could almost hear them silently asking the other how such a clown had managed to make it onto a Jonniee fashion shoot. If only they knew that the gorgeous clothes they were modelling were her own. But of course, she could never tell them so — she needed to remain as anonymous as possible for the time being.

'Now, slowly, slowly, take off the robe. No, one shoulder at a time,' Phil snapped, unable to keep the impatience out of his voice.

Payne stirred, aware of a dark anger building up inside him. He wanted to stalk across there and tell Jinx to keep her catty comments to herself. Wanted to yank the photographer aside by the scruff of his neck and ask him if he couldn't see for himself that Charmaine was terrified. What she needed was patience and confidence-boosting encouragement. Not more hassle.

The robe slithered to her feet, where it pooled like pale cream, revealing a simple but stunning cream and apricot one-piece bathing suit. The sea caught the robe, but since Jo-Jo didn't seem to care that the precious merchandise was getting ruined, neither did Phil, who took the opportunity to take some fantastic shots of the silken robe, the silken model, and the restless sea foaming at her feet.

'OK. Fizz, you're next. I want you cavorting in the surf for this, so make sure you wear something that'll actually take salt water. Jo-Jo, you included some, right?'

Jo-Jo nodded, but could have told him that Charmaine, as chief designer, always insisted on the right materials for the right job, and had always maintained that the people who bought her clothes actually expected their swimwear to allow them to swim! It was only Jo-Jo who designed for the true beach bunnies who only wanted to look good on sun loungers.

Charmaine walked quickly away, her relief on escaping clear for all to see.

Payne watched her approach the changing area, scowling ferociously. If having her picture taken was such a nightmare

for her, why was she doing it? Did she crave fame and ado-
ration so much? Was she out to snare a rich husband, and
thought the glamour of being a fashion model might help
her make it happen? Or did she just want the jet-set lifestyle,
the shoots in the Bahamas, the après-ski in Aspen, the yacht
on the Mediterranean?

'The photographer looked pleased,' he said, walking up
to the edge of a bed sheet. He slowly raised one amused brow
as she snatched up a huge fluffy beach towel and pulled it
around her.

'I'm sorry?' she said coolly, wishing she'd known he was
there. How long had he been watching? Had he really seen
her make such a fool of herself?

'The photographer. I was watching him. He might have
sounded put out for the most part, but once or twice there,
he looked positively radiant.'

Charmaine's eyes hardened. 'There's no need to be sar-
castic. I know he couldn't wait to get rid of me.'

It was true that he'd only lingered on her shots for five
minutes or so, whereas the others had had at least twenty
minutes.

Payne shrugged. 'If you want to put yourself down all
the time . . .' he let his voice trail off suggestively.

Charmaine bit her lip. 'Look, you, I don't care—'

'Mind the lipstick,' Payne interrupted chidingly, and
then laughed as her fists closed in temper. No doubt she'd
have liked to kick his shins again, but he already had a bruise
there, and wasn't about to give her the chance to give him
any more, thank you very much.

'You know, you look like an outraged kitten when you
scowl like that. What's the matter, did someone take away
your bowl of cream?'

'Oh, go to hell,' Charmaine muttered, turning her back
on him.

Suddenly, she felt two warm lips on the top of her right
shoulder, the contact shooting down through her bones like
liquid lightning, grounding her to the floor. She staggered

31

forward, spinning in outrage, aware that, under the concealing terry-cloth of the towel, her nipples had tightened into hard, tingling buds.

'How d-dare you,' she gulped.

He was looking utterly innocent. 'How dare I what?'

She blinked. Had she imaged that feather-light kiss? She gulped. Even worse, had she secretly been craving such a caress, such public acknowledgement of his desire for her, that she'd imagined it?

'Didn't you just . . . touch my shoulder?' she asked breathlessly.

Payne smiled. 'Oh yes,' he said softly, with such evident self-satisfaction she gaped. 'And very lovely it was too. Just a taste of sea salt, warm, smooth, as creamy as that bathing suit you're still wearing.'

His eyes, his grey, fathomless eyes, seemed to draw her in, in and down, drowning her in the desire to feel those lips again. On the side of her neck. Nibbling her earlobe. On the cusp of her breasts, sucking on her now painful nipples, running down her stomach, his tongue dipping into her navel . . .

She drew in a long, shuddering breath. 'I think you're despicable,' she finally managed. 'Just because we're models, it doesn't mean we're there for you men just to . . . just to . . .' but she couldn't actually get the words out. She'd watched his eyebrow rise higher and higher in amusement at her outburst and now she was so angry she was incoherent.

'Oh, but I don't want to "just to, just to" with any other girl but you,' he mocked. 'Doesn't that make a difference?'

And, before she could angrily deny that it made any difference at all, he stepped closer, straining against the flimsy bed-sheet cordon and threatening to knock it over, his hand reaching over the top to cup her chin in his palm. 'Doesn't that make a difference, Charmaine?' he demanded huskily, his eyes on her trembling lips.

Charmaine gulped. Her skin felt on fire where his finger and thumb held her in a firm grip. His eyes once more threatened to sink her, and it was all she could do to step back, tearing herself from his grip.

'N-no,' she managed to rasp, although her voice would have carried much more authority if it hadn't been so weak and tremulous. 'No, it makes no difference. You can't just go around kissing girls on the shoulders when they're not looking.'

'How about when they are?' he purred, and she gave a yelp.

'Don't you dare,' she warned, at the same time as Jo-Jo called over, 'Charmaine, you're up again.'

He noticed Payne and moved across to them, holding the next garment in his hands. 'Payne, good to see you again,' he said, his eyes moving speculatively from Charmaine and back to the casino owner. He could have sliced the atmosphere with a machete. Well, well! His eyes gleamed with interest. Was his shy partner finally coming out of her shell at last?

Payne, Charmaine noticed angrily, was now stood back from the changing area, and looking as if butter wouldn't melt.

'Hello. I just thought I'd come down and see if you wanted any extras for your fashion shoot at the Palace. You know, croupiers, waitresses. Real staff, real people. Or if you want the place deserted. As you know, I can only close the gambling rooms off for an hour,' he said, all friendly and business-like.

Liar, liar, pants on fire, Charmaine thought childishly. He'd only come down so he could ogle the girls, just like the rest of the entire beach's male population.

'Oh I don't know. I'll ask Phil. My immediate thoughts are that we won't want anybody close up, but maybe as a wide room shot — perhaps with all five girls at a gaming table each. Hmm, food for thought. Oh, babe, here,' he added, handing Charmaine what seemed to be a handkerchief.

It was, in fact, a pair of shimmering gold bikini briefs. 'Where's the bikini top. You know, the brassiere part?' she asked. This wasn't one of her designs, but one of Jo-Jo's.

'There isn't one for this shot,' Jo-Jo said, then abruptly realised his mistake. He'd picked up the wrong outfit. This one had never been meant for her at all.

Charmaine looked ready to faint.

She felt ready to faint.

Go topless? In front of all these people. In front of Payne? She knew Phil would photograph her tastefully, with nothing explicit appearing in the final images, but that didn't help her in this moment. She shot stricken, help-me eyes at Jo-Jo. At the same time, Jinx, having spotted Payne, was all but running up the beach behind her, her eyes riveted to the gold scrap of material.

'I can't wear that,' Charmaine whispered, as Payne took an instinctive step closer to her. She looked so pale, he thought she was actually going to pass out.

'Oh, for pity's sake, give it to me,' Jinx hissed, smiling sneeringly at Charmaine. 'Jo-Jo, you shouldn't go teasing the amateur talent,' she added, even more devastatingly.

To Payne's surprise, Charmaine seemed to agree. 'Yes, Jo-Jo, Jinx must wear it. It's far more her colour than mine.'

And then, puzzling him even more, Jo-Jo nodded eagerly.

Payne watched the look of shared relief pass between Charmaine and Jo-Jo as Jinx triumphantly swanned off with the prize garment, but not before casting a gloating look in Charmaine's direction, and a much more flirtatious one in his, which he ignored completely.

Payne looked suspiciously from Jo-Jo to Charmaine. He had no doubts now that Jo-Jo was gay — he'd seen him flirting shamelessly with a male beach attendant not ten minutes ago. So if Charmaine wasn't sleeping with him, why was the owner of Jonniee so anxious to please her?

'I'd better go make sure Phil doesn't go overboard on the close-ups,' Jo-Jo said wryly. 'We're not filming for *Penthouse*.'

Charmaine laughed with utter relief. Then jumped as Payne Lacey tapped her on the shoulder. She spun around, chin up, eyes spitting, an Amazon ready to commence battle.

'Want to tell me what's going on?' he said mildly.

Charmaine felt her blood chill. 'What do you mean?'

'I mean, what's going on,' he repeated with heavy patience. 'You've obviously never modelled before in your life, even I can tell that. And no real fashion model would have passed up a chance to model the star exhibit. And Jo-Jo treats you like bone china.' He smiled grimly. 'What's the matter, Charmaine? Speechless? Do you think I'm so brainless that I can't tell when something's off? And something's off here, sweetheart, by a mile. So tell me. Why are you really in the Bahamas?'

Charmaine stared at him helplessly. What to say? What to do? She couldn't tell him who she really was. Luckily, she and Lucy didn't share the same last name, so there was no reason for him to suspect her true identity. But she had to distract him somehow.

And she could only think of one way.

Taking a bold step forward, she smiled lazily.

'That's for me to know and you to find out,' she said, then reached over the top of the bed sheet to loop her arms around his neck, dragged his head down to hers, and kissed him.

Hard.

CHAPTER FOUR

The moment her lips touched his, Charmaine knew she was in trouble. Deep trouble.

A sigh broke from her, was taken up by Payne, and suddenly the air was molten! She felt his tongue push her lips apart and he raised one hand to cup the back of her head, capturing her in a dominant embrace, as if afraid she might pull away. Liquid heat surged into her body as their lips fused. She moaned and felt her legs tremble beneath her, threatening to give way and dump her ignominiously into the sand.

As if he was aware of her sudden weakness, she felt his other arm come around her waist, pulling her towards him, trapping her against the rock-solid length of his body. One of the poles was ripped out of the sand, letting the sheet fall to the ground and enabling him to pull her even more closely into his embrace.

Her nipples flared into tingling life as they were crushed against his hard masculine chest. She clung to him as the kiss deepened and deepened, threatening to drag her down into a whirlpool of sensation.

Stop it! Stop it! A little voice of sheer panic suddenly piped up in the back of her head. Isn't this exactly what must have happened to Lucy? This mad desire to give herself over to the man, regardless of the consequences? Hadn't this wonderful folly been the start of all her sister's heartache?

Wrenching her head painfully free of his hand and dragging her lips from his in an act of sheer hard-won willpower, she managed to take a step backwards. This made him stagger forwards before his superb sense of balance reasserted itself.

His eyes, which had been closed, suddenly snapped open to gaze at her, their grey stormy depths looking both heart-wrenchingly drugged and yet puzzled.

'What's wrong?' he murmured softly, a small smile playing with his hard, cruel mouth. 'Don't try and tell me you didn't like it.'

Charmaine dragged in a breath, then another, unaware that it made her breasts heave beneath the inadequate covering of the swimsuit. Unconsciously, she rubbed the back of her hand across her mouth, trying in vain to wipe away the residue of his kiss but succeeding only in making his eyes flash a warning, his irises the cold steel colour of a rapier.

But she didn't notice his hurt anger as she shook her head helplessly from side to side.

No, this mustn't happen to her. Not now. Not with this man, of all men.

'No,' she said out loud, unaware she'd voiced her fears into actual words.

'No?' Payne said harshly, the sleepy, amused look fading completely from his eyes. 'No?' he repeated softly, dangerously. 'Then perhaps, if kissing disgusts you so much,' he grated, 'you shouldn't go around kissing men willy nilly. It tends to give us the wrong idea.'

And with that he gave her a crooked, sardonic smile and walked away.

It wrenched at her heart to see him go, which in turn, made her go cold with fear. What kind of a hold did he have over her? And how had it happened? Because only people you cared about could hurt you like that.

Charmaine clutched the fallen sheet closer to her and looked around wildly, but fortunately, everyone was concentrating on the photo shoot.

All except for Jinx, who looked daggers at her.

* * *

The hotel boasted a small garden, but at two o'clock that afternoon, with the sun at its hottest, everybody was either swimming in the coolness of the sea, or taking a much-needed siesta.

However, Charmaine, who was too restless to sleep after the trials and tribulations of that morning's session, drifted about the flowerbeds, redolent with hibiscus and jasmine, and slowly meandered towards the big hedge bordering the Palace, with its promise of shade and cool grass. There she sank down onto the lawn with a weary sigh, and leant against the coolness of the green foliage with a worried expression troubling her lovely face.

How had things disintegrated so far, and how was she ever going to salvage them? Payne Lacey must think she was positively insane! First she kisses him, then she reacts like a wronged maiden in a Gothic romance. And if the withering look he'd given her before he'd stormed off had been any indication, he was going to give her a very wide berth from now on.

After all, it wasn't as if he didn't have his pick of beautiful women with which to console himself. Jinx, for one, was on the lookout for a new lover. Even Charmaine could read the signs that said as much! She sighed again, then started as she heard his voice. It was as if thinking about him had conjured him up from the ether, and she tensed, instinctively wanting to run, until she told herself not to be so silly. He was obviously working in his precious gardens next door, and couldn't possibly see her. The hedge was far too thick.

'I don't care. I don't like being made a fool of.' He sounded angry, and she wondered, grimly, if he was rehearsing what he might want to say to her the next time they met.

But the voice that answered him was definitely male and, what's more, placatory.

'I know, I know, I've said I'm sorry. I never thought the gossip would spread so far.'

'Oh come on, you know how the jungle drums work on this island.'

'Sorry. Look, it got out of hand.'

'I'll say!' Payne gritted, and behind the covering screen of leaves, Charmaine winced in sympathy for whoever was feeling the edge of his tongue. Payne Lacey in a temper must be a frightening sight.

'Next time, don't drag me into your affairs.'

'All right. Look, don't go on so. I'm sorting it out.'

'I should hope so. Your wife deserves that, at least,' Payne all but snapped.

'Let's leave Maria out of this, shall we? You know things between us are a bit . . . fraught at the moment.'

Charmaine frowned. What was this? Was she actually hearing Payne Lacey, Payne Lacey of all men, defending a woman? And a wronged wife, no less, by the sound of things. Surely that couldn't be? The perpetual playboy, the love-them-and-leave-them Lothario of the Bahamas?

Charmaine shook her head. It made no sense. And yet, he'd sounded genuinely angry and genuinely concerned for the unknown 'Maria'.

Yet again she felt uneasy, as the man she knew she must hate once more showed her the unexpectedly honourable and considerate side of his nature.

'And whose fault is that?' Payne said sharply. 'If your marriage is on the rocks, you have no one to blame but yourself.'

Ah, now that was more the kind of thing she'd expect from him, Charmaine thought, with a sour smile. The man was pitiless.

'OK, OK. Anyway, I'm flying to England tomorrow. This situation has gone on long enough,' his friend replied tersely.

They must have walked slowly away after that, for Charmaine could barely make out Payne's response. Then the sound of their voices faded completely.

For a few moments, she continued to sit in the shade, miserably aware that her heart was beating like a drum, her palms were sweating, and she was gulping in air like a beached fish. And all because of his voice. Just because she knew he'd been there, just a few inches away.

Good grief, she had to get herself under control. He was the one who was supposed to be feeling all uneasy and giddy with desire. Not her! She was supposed to remain cool and calm and calculating.

She had to stop this melting feeling of desire every time he came near her. It would be disastrous if she fell into the same trap as Lucy. Worse than disastrous, because she'd have absolutely no excuse — she'd be doing it with her eyes wide open!

* * *

That night, Charmaine dressed with extra care. They were all once more going to the Palace, but this time Phil and his helpers were eager to get some preliminary shots of the venue, so he could get an artistic take on the background. Usually casinos didn't allow photographs to be taken inside the building, since the security men were always alert to potential robbers trying to 'case' the building, and management was always on the lookout for potential gamblers trying to work out how to beat the system, but Jo-Jo had reassured Payne that he could have all the negatives taken that night, so there was no risk.

But Charmaine wasn't so much interested in work, but in how to repair the damage done that morning. And she knew she would have to look particularly stunning to win back Payne's favour.

She chose a tube of electric-blue silk shot through with silver as the opening salvo in the battle. One of her more daring creations, it was literally a tube of material, hanging from silver straps and falling to mid-calf. All the shape came from the body underneath. When designing it, Charmaine had stipulated it must be made from raw silk, which would cling in all the places it touched, giving it form. The swirling threads of silver made it sparkle in the light. With her pale blue eyes and her silvery hair hanging down past her shoulders, it was perfect.

With it she wore strappy silver sandals and gorgeous, pagan-looking beaten silver and aquamarine jewellery.

If this didn't make him want to give her a second chance, she didn't know what would.

* * *

Payne was watching a Japanese businessman lose his last hundred thousand dollars when they walked through the door.

The photographer immediately began snapping film, and he was amused to note that, even though they weren't for publication, Jinx managed to get in some of the shots. The redhead was wearing deep royal purple, a mere scrap of satin that barely covered her. Once he was sure that Charmaine had noticed him watching Jinx woo and charm (and yes, even manage to distract) some of the dedicated gamblers, he turned at last and let his eyes run boldly over her from top to bottom.

He hoped, from where she stood across the room of baccarat players, that she couldn't see the way his breath caught in his lungs, or the sweat that popped out on his forehead.

Not that any red-blooded male would have reacted differently. She looked simply magnificent. Under the light of the chandeliers, the silver in her dress caught and flashed at him, as if signalling him in some code known only to lovers. It was certainly pulling him across the room as if she were a magnet, and he a mere iron filing. The rest of his body was feeling iron hard too, and he cursed this instant effect she had on him.

He was going to have to be very careful around this woman. She was the human equivalent of dynamite!

'Hello, Payne,' Jo-Jo said as he bore down on them, admiring the cut of the other man's dinner jacket. He wished he looked as good in tropical white. 'Thanks for this,' he said, indicating the happily snapping photographer. 'I promise you he won't disturb the gamblers.'

'No trouble,' Payne said briefly, then snapped his fingers at a hovering waiter. 'And speaking of gambling,' he said, smiling, 'I thought the ladies might like a flutter.'

And with that the waiter lowered the tray, revealing not fluted glasses of champagne, but piles of chips — red, black, green and white.

Jinx, of course, was immediately there. 'Payne, for us!' she breathed, widening her eyes and rubbing her arm against his. 'How deliciously wicked.'

The other girls murmured too. Even the chronically bored Coral perked up. 'Lovely. I must try my hand at poker,' she said, reaching out and grabbing a handful. 'I've always wanted to!'

By the time the others had done the same there were very few chips left.

Charmaine couldn't have cared if they'd taken them all. Gambling just wasn't her thing. Besides, she was still trying to find her tongue and come up with a good opening line for Payne. 'Sorry I kissed you' just didn't seem appropriate somehow.

'The greedy little darlings,' Jo-Jo drawled ruefully, watching his models eagerly making for the various tables, and then reached for the few meagre specimens left on the tray. Wryly he handed them over to Charmaine, who had no choice but to let him drop them into her hand.

'Oh no, Jo-Jo,' she murmured, looking uncomfortable. 'Why don't you take them. You're bound to have more luck than me.'

'Oh I don't know,' Payne said softly. 'Sometimes Lady Luck recognises one of her sisters.'

Charmaine forced her eyes up to meet his. She tried for a puzzled yet sophisticated glance.

'Oh?'

'Another Lady I mean,' he said softly. 'Lady Bountiful, perhaps?' he teased. 'Or maybe Lady Godiva. With that wonderful blonde hair . . .'

Charmaine blinked. Wasn't Lady Godiva known for riding around naked on a white horse? She almost snorted. He should be so lucky!

Payne, eyes twinkling in response to her angry flush, reached out to push back a soft strand of hair from her cheek.

It was all she could do to stand still.

Beside her, she heard Jo-Jo give a soft sigh. He'd always been a romantic. And so must she be, if she was ever going to get Payne Lacey back in her sights, she reminded herself grimly. It was no good just standing there like a statue, she reprimanded herself.

'How kind,' she said softly. 'But I've never placed a bet in my life. I'm not sure I know how.' She hoped she sounded as helpless as a lost kitten. It was, she was almost sure, the kind of thing Jinx would say, if she wanted to encourage a man to show how big and strong and gallant he was.

Then she saw Payne's lips twitch in amusement, and wondered if she hadn't overdone it somewhat.

'Well then in that case,' he said, offering her his arm, 'allow me to demonstrate.'

She tensed as she slipped her hand through the crook of his arm, and knew, without having to look up at him, that he was grinning like the devil at her.

Of course he'd seen right through her little-girl act the moment the words were out of her mouth. It was no use. She was just no good at this sort of thing. Still, at least he was by her side, and hadn't simply gone off with Jinx. Which must mean that she hadn't totally put him off with her stupid behaviour this morning.

Unless, of course, he was just waiting for a chance to get his revenge.

She looked up at him nervously, but his face was calm and alert. She looked around, seeing the place through his eyes. Yes, she could see why there was such pride of ownership in his countenance. This was his kingdom. A man who could gamble everything he owned, and win, would be king here forever.

He led her towards the gaming tables. Over to her right, she heard Dee-Dee mock moan as she lost at cards.

'Does the bank always win?' Charmaine asked cynically.

Payne gave a wolfish grin. 'The odds always favour the house, of course,' he said simply, 'otherwise there'd be no casinos. We'd all go bankrupt. But the lure is in beating the odds. Occasionally there are big winners, which only encourages the others.'

'Has anyone ever broken the bank here?' she asked, and Payne gave a cold, hard smile.

'No,' he said simply.

No. Of course not, Charmaine thought sourly. As if anyone would dare!

'Here were are,' he said, moving up to a table containing a roulette wheel. A woman who was not playing but only watching quickly made way for him. The man behind the wheel, resplendent in the Palace uniform of gold waistcoat, red bow tie, crisp white shirt and black trousers, looked up anxiously at his employer, but Payne merely smiled.

His hand came to rest on the small of Charmaine's back, making a long, sensuous shudder travel the length of her spine.

She hoped he didn't notice.

At the same time, her breath became trapped in her throat as the heat of his casually resting fingertips burned through the fabric of her dress, and her nipples hardened and tightened like little tell-tales in the clinging, revealing dress.

Don't let him notice that either, she thought frantically. Oh please!

She coughed, managing to dislodge her breath, and plastered a false smile onto her face. 'So, what do I do?' she asked brightly. And looked up to find him staring down at her, his eyes dreamily caressing the curve of her breast.

'Hmm? Oh, with the chips you mean,' he teased, watching yet again as she blushed in mortification.

Really, he must stop doing this to her. But it was so hard to resist. He did so love the way her icy, sometimes frightening beauty melted so charmingly into consternation.

'Yes,' Charmaine gritted. 'You were going to teach me to play roulette, remember?'

This man was a monster! He knew exactly what a hold he had over women, and used it with all the skill of a surgeon wielding a knife. No wonder poor Lucy had been unable to resist him.

He was like a drug. Even now, as mad as she was with him, as humiliated and flustered, she was aware of the sharp pine tang of his aftershave. The smooth line of his jaw, freshly shaved, and the firm moulded line of his lips. She wanted to kiss him again. To be prepared this time, for the devastation of his mouth on hers — to revel in it, in fact.

Yes, she had no doubt loving this man would be an experience like no other. The surrender of mind and body to another, a giving over of the entire self to bliss.

Ah, but afterwards. When the drug was withdrawn, leaving a soul craving more . . . No, she must never succumb. He had to pay for what he'd done so callously to Lucy, and who knew how many others.

'The wheel is on the table,' Payne pointed out dryly, making the woman who'd moved over and several other gamblers sitting around the table laugh softly.

Her face flamed. Damn him! She'd been staring up at him like a moonstruck calf!

She didn't realise it, but nobody was actually laughing at her. In fact, the men at the table were all looking at her appreciatively, and envying the casino owner his companion, while the woman who'd been usurped at the table sighed enviously. An older woman, dripping in diamonds, looked positively misty-eyed, sensing young love, and perhaps remembering past loves of her own.

But to Charmaine she felt as if she was suddenly the butt of everyone's joke.

'What do I do?' she asked grimly, trying to smile, but wanting only to run and hide.

'Well, you can bet on either black or red, but it doesn't pay very well. Or you can bet on a specific number.'

'Fourteen,' she said promptly, the date of her birthday in February.

'You've got to part with one of your chips, sweetheart,' he murmured, raising her clenched fist with one hand and kissing the back of her knuckles. 'Not even at the Palace do we bet with nothing but thin air.'

Again a ripple of indulgent laughter came from the others and she abruptly opened her palm, allowing him to pick out a single chip. She wanted to curl her fingers back into a fist and . . .

His eyes crinkled at the corners, and she could almost believe he could read her mind.

He reached forward and placed the chip on the fourteen square. The others had already made their bets, and with far less fuss, and the croupier spun the wheel.

All eyes turned to the spinning centrepiece, as if it held the answer to all of life's mysteries.

All except her own gaze. She knew the odds of the ball falling into her own slot were almost astronomical. Instead she looked up at the man beside her. 'Do you ever play?' she asked.

'Yes, but not here,' he said softly. 'There'd be no thrill,' he explained at her puzzled look. 'If I lose I haven't really lost because the money returns to me. And if I win, I haven't really won, because it's my own money returning to me. No, when I gamble, I go to Monaco.'

Charmaine smiled dryly. Of course he did. What was she thinking of, even asking him?

'And what did you win there? A yacht? A beach house?' A woman?

Payne shrugged, a small secretive smile pulling at his lips.

Yes, it was a woman, she thought. She wouldn't put it past him. She wouldn't put anything past him.

A sudden wave of congratulation rent the tense air, and she turned back, confused, towards the table.

'You win,' Payne said, and her eyes shot to the small white ball, nestling in the fourteen slot.

'I won?' she echoed numbly.

The croupier, smiling, pushed across the table a small pile of chips.

'Want to bet the whole lot on another roll?' Payne asked, but she was already gathering them up.

'Oh no,' she said, laughing gaily. 'That was pure beginner's luck and I know enough to quit when I'm ahead.'

'Do you,' he said softly, something in his voice making her head rise sharply, her gaze cannoning into his own. 'Do you really?'

Her lips fell open in shock as she realised she'd somehow wandered into a minefield.

'The casino owner's worst nightmare,' Payne drawled softly. 'A lucky gambler who knows when to quit.'

Everyone laughed except Charmaine. Her heart was beating too loud, and was seemingly lodged in her throat, preventing even a minor giggle. His eyes were drowning her. The very air seemed thick with portent. What did he mean? What was happening?

'In that case, I'd better get what I can out of it,' Payne smiled wolfishly. 'If you're going to run off with the house profits, I demand a thank-you kiss.'

Charmaine blinked. He what?

The crowd around the table burst into laughter and applause as Payne stepped closer, looped one arm around her waist and pulled her close.

As his head bent over hers, he whispered wickedly, so that only she could hear. 'This time, it's my turn.'

And then he was kissing her.

CHAPTER FIVE

As she watched his head swooping low over hers, his eyes glittering with sardonic amusement at her obvious panic, Charmaine told herself that this time she would be ready for him. That this time his kiss would not totally undo her. There would be no humiliating loss of strength in her knees, no overwhelming pounding of her heart blotting out all other sounds.

This time, it would be different. It had to be. Her very sanity depended on it.

His lips touched hers and she stiffened. Vaguely, very vaguely, she was aware of the amused laughter of the other guests. She tried hard to hold onto that thought — that they were in a public place when all was said and done, and that he was only kissing her out of a sense of mischief. Surely these two facts were enough to keep her on the straight and narrow.

But it was impossible. A moment later, his tongue gently teased her lips apart, and his fingers splayed against her back, radiating a sense of desire that seeped into her spine, turning her bones to mush. All too soon, and with a dreadful sense of déjà vu, she felt her body flare into life, as if it were a firework, and Payne the lighted taper.

She tried to push against him, but he was like rock — immovable, solid and unyielding. She might have whimpered against his marauding lips, or perhaps some hidden sense of chivalry pierced his conscience, but just when she thought she was going to lose herself completely, he lifted his head. She thought she heard him drag in a ragged, shaken breath, but knew she must have been mistaken.

A man like Payne Lacey wasn't going to find a simple kiss as devastating or as soul-shaking as she did herself.

She forced her eyes open, unaware until that moment that they must have feathered closed. When had that happened?

Payne looked down into pale blue eyes filled with stars, as well as anger and . . . yes, fear. Not that he could blame her for feeling so bewildered. He too felt in need of a stiff drink.

'Well worth the loss of house profits,' he forced himself to say lightly, making their audience laugh in appreciation. Then the croupier called for the placing of bets, and instantly they were forgotten as, once more, all eyes turned to the enchanted wheel.

'Come on, this way,' Payne said dryly, taking her elbow in a firm grip. She looked so vulnerable and in need of rescuing that he wanted nothing more than to take her far away from the hard heat and the indefatigable glamour that was the casino. For the first time in years, Payne felt almost ashamed of his empire.

She nearly stumbled, so unnerved was she by the sensation of warm, hard, strong fingers taking control of her. What would it be like to feel those fingers touch other parts of her, she wondered. Softly, gently caressing . . .

No. No, no, no! She must stop this madness now, at once.

'Where are we going?' she gulped, glancing over her shoulder, where Jo-Jo was staring after her, an amazed look on his face. She knew just how he felt! If her business partner had never thought to see her kissing a handsome playboy in public, how much less had she herself ever dreamed of such a possibility?

Things were going too fast.

All right, in a way she was pleased that her plan was back on track. At least Payne was showing a flattering amount of interest again. But on the other hand, she felt as if she were juggling with explosives. One fumbled drop and boom! And she'd be the one blown to pieces, with her heart a major casualty.

And, deep down inside, she knew she just didn't have the flair for this kind of juggling.

'I thought I'd show you the conservatory,' Payne replied softly. 'There's an orchid I've been cultivating that I want you to see. If it's successful I have to find a name for it. How about Charmaine's Delight? Or Charmaine's Desire?'

His voice was low and husky now, and doing things to her skin. She could feel every pore of her body quiver at the sexy timbre of it.

The man positively exuded sex appeal. Deep, dark sex appeal.

She couldn't possibly go into the conservatory with him. With the velvet night pressing against the glass, the twinkling diamonds of the stars above, and the heady scent of orchids wafting across the night air, she'd lose her head completely!

But how to get out of it?

It was Jinx, of all people, who came to her rescue. Perhaps she'd seen the kiss, or had merely sensed the charged atmosphere and felt obliged to reclaim her authority, but she suddenly appeared in front of them, and determinedly looped one arm through Payne's.

'Darling, I've lost all my chips,' she pouted prettily. 'I need some more.'

Payne smiled dryly. Wouldn't she always?

He turned just too late to stop Charmaine slipping away. He watched her go, all but bolting like a startled fawn, back into the crowd, and smiled darkly.

She could run, but she couldn't hide.

As Jinx began to wheedle and flirt shamelessly, he told himself that Charmaine Reece had better make the most of her reprieve.

She would not get another one.

* * *

Charmaine climbed anxiously onto the dark blue table. Unlike most other casinos, the Palace had felt and baize gaming tables in colours other than dark green — most notably navy blue, deep cream, crimson and gold.

For the first full photoshoot inside the Palace, Charmaine was wearing an exquisitely cut creation in mushroom satin. Reminiscent of slinky nightdresses and floating peignoirs, it had Bruges lace at the throat and wrists, and fell in plain, lush folds, almost to her feet.

It was mid-afternoon, but because the inner gaming rooms had no windows at all, Phil had been able to make good use of lighting to create an atmosphere of night-time elegance. Coloured candles and old-fashioned lanterns supplanted the casino's usual harsh electric lighting.

Phil wanted Charmaine photographed lying on the baccarat table. Her long silvery gold hair was unconfined and spilled around her shoulders, across the dress and over the dark blue table top, in fabulous contrast.

Dee-Dee had been first up, dressed in dazzling white and draped around a slot machine like a pole dancer. It had been very sexy, and was definitely a hard act to follow.

Now, as she concentrated nervously on Phil's demands to 'think like a siren', Charmaine tried to ignore the blond Adonis-like figure of Payne Lacey standing at the back of the room.

'Right, now half-close your eyes. Imagine you've just spotted your lover across a crowded room, and you're sending him come-to-bed messages,' Phil said, crouching to get a shot of her at table-height.

A soft flush crept over Charmaine's face as she tried to keep her eyes from straying towards the back. Why, oh why, had Phil used that particular instruction!

'Come on, Charmaine, think sensuous!' Phil encouraged. At the moment she looked more hunted than amorous.

She heard Coral say something and one of the other girls laugh. She was blowing it again. Even Jo-Jo stirred restlessly.

Damn it, Charmaine thought with a sudden flash of anger, I'll show them. I won't ruin another good photoshoot.

I won't! She owed Jo-Jo, and herself too, more than that. Think about a lover, Phil had said. Well, all right then. She would! Deliberately, she let her eyes stray to those of Payne Lacey. It was not exactly hard to do, since they seemed to be drawn there anyway, like one of those hapless heroines in a vampire movie on the first appearance of the Count!

She stretched one arm further away, lowering her head closer to the table. She imagined him walking closer, like a wolf, silent and loping. He would lean down, perhaps pull a swathe of hair off her shoulder and bend to kiss the exposed flesh.

Phil began to snap like a man demented, his mind racing. Whatever it was he'd said to her, she'd certainly taken it to heart! This was sensational stuff!

Charmaine felt a dreamy smile come to her lips as she imagined his first tender kiss — perhaps on the curve of her shoulder, or the small indent on her neck. She almost shuddered at the imagined touch.

He'd say her name, softly. She'd turn onto her back and look up at him. Without thinking she did so, and Phil leapt up onto the bench placed beside the table for just such a shot. He didn't care that he hadn't asked her for the pose — he knew when a model was going with the flow, and he was more than happy to go with her.

Especially when she was producing such stunning shots as this.

Those electric-blue eyes, narrowing to icy slits then opening wide with languorous desire, were so hot that he felt sure he was getting images that would make even the negatives sizzle!

Over on the other side of the room, Payne Lacey felt himself harden and burn, and cursed silently. What did she think she was playing at? Everything had fallen silent as all the people in the room became aware of the sensation taking place on the baccarat table.

His hands curled into fists, his fingernails digging into his palms. He wanted to go over there and ravish her on the spot. And at the same time give her a tongue-lashing for acting the wanton.

Charmaine sighed, looking up at Phil, but seeing only Payne. Since she would never in reality let him touch her as she was imagining his touch, where was the harm?

She stretched, arching her back, imagining his hands on her breasts, cupping, caressing, moving around and down to take the tender line of her hips in his hands. Slowly, slowly, lowering his head to kiss the waiting, quivering skin between her breasts.

'Great, that's it,' Phil said, suddenly snapping her rudely back into reality. She shot up, scrambling off the table, knowing her face must be even more scarlet than Jinx's mini cocktail dress.

This was awful. She'd never be able to show her face again. What had come over her?

'Right, Jinx — I think we'll have you rolling dice,' Phil said, his voice utterly matter-of-fact and professional, and doing much to dispel the sex-laden atmosphere, while Charmaine scurried for cover and the relative peace of the changing rooms.

Two men followed her.

First Jo-Jo, and, after a pause, and far more discreetly, the tall, blond figure of the richest man in the Bahamas.

A small office had doubled as the girls' changing room, and was for the moment deserted. The make-up girls and dressers were all in the casino, watching the shoot.

She carefully slipped her lovely gown from her body, and wrapped herself into a warm cotton housecoat. She was shaking all over.

What must the others be thinking of her now?

Damn that man, Payne Lacey. Even his imaginary self was enough to make her act like a wanton harlot. Worse, a wanton idiot.

A knock at the door made her shoot off the chair. Warily Jo-Jo poked his head inside. 'You decent?' he asked, one hand covering his eyes.

Charmaine laughed dryly. 'Hardly. Or did you miss the performance?' she said, not quite managing to cover the real shame in her voice with a flippant tone.

Jo-Jo came further inside, letting the door close behind him. The door, made of heavy oak, didn't quite catch, and creaked open an inch or so. Outside, in the deserted corridor, Payne had just managed to catch her words, and the reprimand which was hovering on his tongue died a thousand deaths.

She sounded so forlorn.

'Oh I could hardly miss it,' Jo-Jo said brightly. 'You were superb. Phil was delighted.'

Charmaine, slumping back down into her chair, looked at her friend and partner helplessly. 'Don't try and make things better,' she admonished. 'I was awful.'

'No, you weren't awful,' Jo-Jo said staunchly. 'Phil wanted you to be really sexy and you were. It wasn't awful at all, but very, very professional.' Then he shrugged. 'But it was so totally unlike you,' he was forced to add honestly. 'Where has my shy and retiring designer gone? And speaking of transformations, what's with you and Payne Lacey?'

Charmaine's head lifted sharply and outside the man himself moved closer.

Yes, what was it, Payne wondered. He would dearly love to know himself.

'What do you mean?' Charmaine said warily, trying to meet Jo-Jo's eyes with a look of innocence. And knowing that she failed.

'Oh come on, love, never kid a kidder,' Jo-Jo said cosily, leaning against the desk the girls were using as a dressing table and looking at his friend closely. 'I've never seen you so aggressive with a man before. You're even giving Jinx a run for her money.'

Charmaine paled. She wasn't being as obvious as all that, surely?

Noting her stricken look, Jo-Jo backed down. 'OK, perhaps you're not coming on that strong,' he amended hastily.

'But for you, it's unheard of. Where's the girl who won't even use her family's famous name to get along? The girl who never dates, but vegetates away in the country like an amateur nun?'

'I don't!' Charmaine said hotly. Then, as Jo-Jo cocked his head to one side, an over-the-top look of scepticism on his face, she felt herself smile.

'Well, I don't vegetate,' she said defensively. 'I create. And I like living in the country.'

'With only a cat for company,' Jo-Jo added.

'Well, Wordsworth's all male,' Charmaine grinned and Jo-Jo rolled his eyes.

'Look, don't get me wrong, love,' he said conspiratorially. 'If you've decided to throw off the shackles of celibacy and go all out for the gorgeous Mr Lacey, I'm all for it. But it's just so . . . sudden. And so unexpected.' His voice became worried. 'Are you sure you know what you're doing?'

And although he didn't say so aloud, he wished she'd chosen someone far less potent than the casino owner on which to test her new-found sexual freedom!

Charmaine couldn't help but laugh. Did she know what she was doing? Not if the past few days were any indication!

'And why were you so determined we shoot here?' Jo-Jo asked, finally voicing the one question which she'd been dreading.

'What? Don't you think it's a fabulous idea?' she asked quickly, trying to distract him. 'Not only have we got the beach and the lush tropics on our doorstep, we've got the Palace as well. I thought you'd be pleased we came.'

'Oh I am,' Jo-Jo said. 'Don't get me wrong. But you've never before dictated the location of a shoot. Usually I have to all but browbeat you into asserting your rights as half-owner of Jonniee. Now, all of a sudden, you're like a dynamo.'

'Oh, don't exaggerate,' Charmaine laughed uneasily. 'I just felt like a change, that's all.'

Outside Payne Lacey, eavesdropping without shame, frowned.

Charmaine Reece was a half-owner of the fashion house? And, by the sound of it, its main designer to boot? It made no sense. And exactly what famous family did she belong to? The more he learned about this dangerous, wonderfully alluring woman, the less he seemed to know her.

'I'm not exaggerating, sweetheart. The changes in you are there for anyone to see. Just a few months ago, you were the epitome of the country mouse, solitary and wary. Now, all of a sudden, you're like a tiger. Even Jinx is beginning to get nervous. For the first time, she's got serious competition. She was certainly spitting fire after that little kiss you and our gorgeous casino owner exchanged at the roulette table last night.'

Charmaine flushed. So everyone had noticed.

'Come on, Jo-Jo. Nobody competes with Jinx,' she said awkwardly. 'She rules!'

Jo-Jo snorted inelegantly and rolled his eyes theatrically. 'Not over Payne Lacey she doesn't. And she knows it. Oh, he tolerates her, and plays up to her. But everyone knows it's you he wants.'

Charmaine felt her world lurch around her.

'He does?' she whispered.

'Of course he does. Isn't that what you want?' Jo-Jo demanded. And outside, their unsuspected eavesdropper echoed the sentiment.

Payne smiled, a wide, wolfish, confident smile. *Yes, Charmaine. Wasn't it what you wanted?*

'I think,' Charmaine took a deep, shaken breath, 'I think this is all nonsense. Now, if you don't mind, the girls will be returning soon for the changes. And I still have to model the green taffeta.'

Jo-Jo took the hint, and when he opened the door, the passageway was empty. But at the door, he turned and looked at his friend, his eyes darkening. 'Be careful, Charmaine, yes?' he said softly. She was so young and innocent. 'Payne Lacey plays in the big leagues.'

Charmaine smiled a grim, hard smile that was totally unlike her. 'Oh, don't worry, Jo-Jo,' she said softly, almost sadly. 'I know what I'm doing.'

But when he was gone, and she was pulling on the rich and voluminous elegance of the green taffeta evening dress, Charmaine wondered if she was trying to convince herself as much as her friend.

* * *

The next day was a day off, as Phil and his assistants were scouting around for a 'jungle' shot, for the day-wear outfits.

With this in mind, Charmaine was glad to slip into a pair of plain white shorts and a pale blue T-shirt, and head out for the day.

Downstairs, in the lobby, she picked up a few leaflets, deciding on a visit to the Garden of the Groves. It was time she did a bit of sightseeing.

She took the bus, using a few of the Bahamian dollars she'd got from the bank. It was crowded with cheerful locals and excited holidaymakers who kept eyeing the beautiful passenger with welcoming smiles.

At the plantation, the gardens were so big that, even though there were plenty of visitors, it felt as if she had her own tropical paradise to herself. For a few hours she wandered around, lost in the verdant greens of the tropical land. Bright scarlet flowers, brilliantly plumed birds, the never-far-away presence of the Caribbean Sea itself, all lulled her with their beauty.

This was truly paradise on earth.

With, she realised a moment later with a lurch of her heart, its own particular brand of serpent.

For a moment she thought she must be seeing things, but no, emerging from a dark patch of shade, walking towards her, a vision in white slacks and shirt, was Payne Lacey.

For a moment, she felt utterly beleaguered. Was she never to be free of this man? The next instant she felt her pulse rate rocket. He was so tall, so lithe, so strong. He was like a sleek golden cat, all power and purrs.

'Are you following me?' she asked him archly, before he could so much as put in a word of greeting.

'You'd like that, wouldn't you?' he drawled right back at her, watching her anger fade and be replaced with a flush of humiliation.

And he wondered yet again how someone so beautiful could be so unsure of herself. In truth he *had* followed her — and he was beginning to think he'd follow her all the way to the moon if that's where she led him. But he wasn't going to let her know that.

'As a matter of fact, one of the gardeners here had a cutting he wanted to give me. For the Palace grounds.'

'Oh,' Charmaine said. Of course. How could she have been so stupid? And how could she expect to wrap this sophisticated man of the world around her little finger when she blurted out such stupid things, and made such basic mistakes?

What would Jinx do now?

'Well, it's nice to know that I take second place to a daisy,' she laughed, hoping her voice came out as husky and seductive as she wanted.

'It's a jasmine actually,' he lied dryly, and let his eyes run over her. 'But you look more lovely than any flower.'

'My, my, how gallant,' she drawled. But didn't quite have the nerve to slip her hand through his arm, as Jinx would have done. Or fish for even more compliments.

'It's beginning to get hot. Shall we go for a cool drink?' he asked, his mocking eyes seeming to read her like a book.

'Sounds wonderful,' she agreed. It was time to take charge. If only she could keep her wayward heart from ruining her plans.

They stopped at a small café overlooking a beautiful bay. Sitting out on the terrace, under huge, gaily striped umbrellas, they watched the bright blue sea sparkling under the noonday sun. Windsurfers, paragliders, water-skiers and speedboat riders made use of the stunning blue waters, while white-capped waves foamed to the shore of perfect white sand.

Payne ordered the drinks, and when the cocktails came, tall, icy-glassed concoctions full of fruit and rum, a tiny replica of the gaily striped umbrella thrust down amongst the ice, Charmaine stared at it in horror.

What was it? And how on earth was one supposed to drink it?

She reached for the little cocktail umbrella and twirled it absently, while looking at the apricot-coloured drink. Did you sip through the ice and fruit, or were you supposed to eat the fruit first?

She knew what Jinx would do — capture Payne's glance, then fish out the fruit with her bare fingers and playfully eat it, letting the juice run down her chin, and challenging him to lick it off . . .

But she couldn't do that. Not even for the sake of her plan. Not even for her beloved Lucy.

Instead she took a tentative sip, then gasped and nearly choked as the rum hit the back of her mouth, with an aftertaste of coconut. Her eyes watered, making them shine like Ceylon sapphires.

Payne watched her, a small, gentle smile playing with his lips.

'You're really not much of a drinker, are you?' he murmured. This woman was nothing if not an enigma. As co-owner of one of the leading fashion houses in the world, she must be rich in her own right. And yet she didn't know how to drink a cocktail. She could have lived in a penthouse in Paris, or a palatial villa in Spain, and yet, according to her friend and business partner, she lived alone in a modest cottage. And apparently didn't even date, let alone play the field, as any other modern, wealthy woman in such a glamorous profession would do.

'They look delicious,' Charmaine said, reaching for a quince-like fruit growing in the wild grounds bordering the terrace. She reached for it, then jumped as Payne shot across the table and grabbed it out of her hand.

'That's poisonous!' he said roughly. 'What's the matter with you, woman, are you trying to kill yourself?' he snarled.

He'd gone white under the tan at the near miss, and Charmaine recoiled from the raw passionate anger in his voice.

'I didn't know! Besides, I wouldn't have eaten it,' she snapped defensively.

Payne shook his head and lobbed the forbidden fruit over the edge, towards the bay. 'I can see I'm going to have to take you in hand. Come on, let's go.'

'Go where?' she asked, glad to abandon her drink and the seductive view of the bay.

'For a tour of the island. I can see I'm going to have to acclimatise you.'

And that wasn't all he wanted to do to her either. But that could wait until darkness had fallen!

Charmaine looked up and saw the smouldering look in his eyes. And once again, felt her world tilt beneath her.

CHAPTER SIX

Still smarting at the way he'd so high-handedly treated her over the poisonous fruit, Charmaine fumed silently as he led her from the gardens and out onto the road, where a low-slung bottle-green Lamborghini was parked.

'Don't tell me. You won this playing poker from an oil tycoon in Texas,' she said ever-so-sweetly, as he opened the door for her. She climbed in, acutely aware of the appreciative glance he was giving her long, bare legs.

'Of course not,' he said softly, closing the door, then leaning down to smile into her eyes. 'I was playing dice in a New York alleyway with a rather dissolute rock and roll star who was rather the worse for drink.'

Charmaine's lips twitched. Really, the man was impossible. And she didn't believe him for an instant.

'I refuse to believe you would take advantage of someone when they were incapacitated,' she said firmly as he folded his long length behind the wheel.

The car, which was already low slung, suddenly became very cramped as he reached forward to turn on the ignition, and when he reached down to put the car in gear, his arm brushed against her leg. Instant heat shot into her, turning her insides liquid.

She drew in a quick, rasping breath. Damn the man, why couldn't he drive one of those big, spacious, modern cars like everyone else?

'Why thank you,' he drawled, pulling away smoothly, the powerful car quickly making short work of the speed limit. 'That's the nicest thing you've said to me so far.'

For a moment, Charmaine was puzzled. Then she understood and bit her lip.

But he was right. So why was she so sure that Payne Lacey wouldn't have all but conned a drunken spoilt rock star out of his prized possession? She shook her head helplessly. Before flying to this island, she would have bet her last penny that that was just the sort of behaviour she could expect from this casino-owning playboy.

Now she would have bet her life against it ever happening.

Then she felt a spurt of anger as she realised she was beginning to see life through his eyes. Bet her life indeed! Payne was the gambler. She was the sensible, normal one. She really must not let him affect her this way. Besides, all it meant was that he had a warped sense of ethics, that was all.

'But you're right,' he said, confusing her all over again, until he looked across at her and grinned widely. 'It was the rock star's manager I was betting against, and he was stone-cold sober. In fact, he has the reputation of having a mind like a steel trap.'

She opened her mouth to ask him what it was he had put up as a bet against this magnificent car, then quickly snapped her lips shut again.

She didn't want to know.

She didn't!

She curled her fingers into fists as she wondered what it could be. Another car. No, that seemed too tame. And surely not his casino or a hotel. She forced herself to look at the passing scenery while Payne shot her another look, a wide grin creasing his handsome face.

'You're just dying to know, aren't you?'

'I am not!' she said hotly. 'Your ridiculous lifestyle affects me not at all. Oh, I expect most people find it glamorous and fascinating, but I'm far more down to earth.'

Payne shot past another car as if it was standing still. Being so low to the ground, it felt as if they were going so fast they would take off at any moment, and Charmaine had to admit she found the sensation thrilling. Terrifying, but thrilling. And yet he was such a superb driver, and the car seemed to be such an extension of his own self, that she never truly felt as if her life was in danger. Or that anyone else on the road need fear them, either.

'So, where would you like to go first?' he asked, as he turned off the main road onto a single lane track which led through sand dunes and tufted grass, the bright azure streak that was the Caribbean Sea playing hide and seek with them as they twisted and turned.

'I don't suppose you've got a bikini on under those very fetching shorts, have you?' he mused, and she glanced nervously down at the expanse of tanned leg she was showing.

'No,' she said truthfully, and with evident relief. At least that was one temptation she wouldn't have to deal with — sunbathing nearly nude on a deserted island beach with this man next to her, looking at her with those wickedly knowing eyes of his.

Payne laughed softly. 'No need to look so pleased about it. Most women like to swim in the warm sea and lay out on the sand under a palm tree.'

Charmaine shrugged one shoulder. 'Not me,' she said firmly. Although it sounded wonderful.

But she wouldn't be able to trust herself. And she certainly couldn't trust this man, of all men, to act the gentleman!

'So, you really are a little miss prim and proper. I know just the activity for you.'

And with that he accelerated away up an even narrower track that climbed higher up onto the top of a high cliff. He pulled the car off road, onto a sandy, grass-compacted stretch of earth, and turned off the engine.

Silence engulfed them for a moment. Then Charmaine heard the susurration of the ever-present sea, the high keening cry of some gulls, and the eerie, moaning lament of the wind. She got out nervously, looking around the deserted terrain. It was a spectacular view, with the rugged rocks and the sea stretching out as far as you could see, but there was not a soul in sight.

What was this?

The wind tugged at her T-shirt as she closed the car door behind her, and rattled her cotton shorts against her derrière. But it was a warm, strong wind, and the sensation wasn't in the least unpleasant.

If only she knew what they were doing here!

She watched him nervously as he moved around to the trunk of the car, opened the boot, and looked at her over the top. 'Tah-dah!' he said, whipping out a bright red, yellow and brown piece of shaped plastic. It took her a moment to recognise it as a kite. A sumptuous, modern, complex kite, shaped like a bird of prey.

'Since even Mary Poppins approved of flying a kite, I felt sure you wouldn't object,' he said cheekily.

Charmaine didn't know whether to laugh or stamp her foot in vexation. All right, so she wasn't another Jinx, and flirting and making love wasn't her forte, but did he really see her as that quintessential, goody-two-shoes English nanny?

And then she frowned. 'Wait a minute. You already had a kite in the boot?'

Payne shrugged but looked just a shade abashed. 'True. My sister and nephew were over here last month, and Adrian, my nephew, was into flying in a big way.' He slammed the boot shut and began to prepare the kite. It looked complicated, with all sorts of strings and pulleys, but soon he had it working. 'The little scamp's only ten, but he could show me a thing or two,' he said, with such exasperated affection in his voice that, for a moment, Charmaine's throat closed up with emotion and she couldn't say a word.

Payne Lacey, the adoring uncle? The richest man for miles, the dedicated gambler, the ultimate playboy, flying a kite with his nephew? How many more unnerving surprises was he going to spring on her?

'Here we go,' he said, turning to run a few steps and launch the multi-coloured eagle into the air. He ran fast and well, turning on a dime, as surefooted as a mountain goat as he twisted and turned to catch the wind currents and raise the bird aloft.

She looked at the edge of the cliff nervously. Had the man no sense of danger at all?

'Want to hold her? I call her Valkyrie.' He held out the two small wooden poles to her, and without a second thought she reached out for them. Immediately she felt the pull and power of the wind as the strings twitched in her hands and the eagle abruptly nosedived, as if mortally wounded.

'Whoa! Keep your arms up — like this,' he said, stepping behind her and taking her hands in his.

Instantly her buttocks tingled as they were pressed into his groin, and her back and shoulders quivered against the hard, muscular planes of his chest and stomach. So intense was her sudden desire for him that she nearly cried out. She very nearly let go of the kite as well. In fact, if his hands hadn't been cupped over hers, guiding the strings, she might well have done.

She gasped, and then tried to disguise her reaction with a laugh. 'It's wonderful,' she said tensely, licking lips gone suddenly dry. 'Who'd have thought flying a kite could be so invigorating?'

And then she felt another kind of hardness, pressing against her derrière, and her face flamed.

Behind her, his lips almost brushing her ear, Payne said dryly, 'Yes. Who'd have thought it.'

What should she do now? Pretend not to notice? Make a saucy comment? She knew what Jinx would do. But she was Charmaine Reece, and was consequently tongue-tied. She took a step forward, breathing a sigh of relief as he let her go. And perhaps feeling just a pang of disappointment?

She jiggled one hand, watching the bird dip and swoop. She mustn't let her perfectly natural physical reaction upset her. It meant nothing. It couldn't mean anything, could it?

'I think I'm getting the hang of this,' she called back over her shoulder, unaware that he was watching her with sardonic, knowing eyes.

'I wouldn't be so sure,' he whispered, his voice almost agonised.

She looked at him over her shoulder, her big blue eyes wide and innocent. 'What?'

He shook his head ruefully. 'Nothing,' he said, sitting down on a clump of grass, willing his body to relax. It was not easy. He wanted her so badly he ached!

His eyes feasted on the sight of her with the kite, the way her shorts curved around her sexy bottom, the way her breasts, unfettered under the T-shirt, bounced and swayed as she ran and turned, watching the kite with undisguised joy, and he shook his head ruefully.

Just what the hell was he supposed to do with this child-woman?

* * *

They stopped for tea, the traditional good old English kind, at a small café. She ordered India, he China, and she was amused to note that fresh baked scones, which her grandmother would be proud to acknowledge as her own, were served with home-made strawberry preserve and clotted cream. They were even seated outside, on surprisingly comfortable ironwork chairs, amidst a glorious garden.

Only the exotic blooms and colourful, darting birds gave away the fact that they were a long way from the Cotswolds or any other equally picturesque but utterly English pastoral location. That and the bright, fierce heat of the afternoon sun. Surely no such sun ever shined in Oxfordshire!

A young and very-much-in-love couple kissed under the shade of a big tree in one corner of the garden, while an old man dozed behind his newspaper at the next table over. Other than these, they had the place to themselves.

'No wonder you chose to live here,' she said softly, watching as a bird, a flash of iridescent green, fed from the nectar of a hibiscus bloom.

'It beats Cardiff on a wet Sunday afternoon,' he agreed, and for the first time Charmaine was able to put a name to that very slight sing-song quality to his voice. So he was Welsh — though given his accent was otherwise American, she guessed he'd spent the majority of his years Stateside before moving to the Bahamas.

She watched him reach forward and spoon a little piece of strawberry preserve and place it on the tip of his finger.

What on earth? She abruptly sat forward on her chair, her heart hammering in her breast. Surely he wasn't going to offer her the morsel? And if he did, would she actually have the nerve to lick it off? She knew that she should. If she was ever to win him over and break his fickle heart, she would have to start luring him somehow.

She swallowed nervously. Could she reach forward, slowly, letting her eyes become dreamy and sensuous, while capturing his wrist lightly in her fingers? A soft sigh feathered past her lips as she could almost feel the hard bone under her caressing fingers, his warm, tanned skin lightly dusted with fine blond hair. He'd catch his breath as she pulled his hand towards her, his own lips parting in desire as she opened her mouth, preparatory to pulling his finger inside.

Her tongue began to tingle in anticipation of licking the sweet jam from his finger, perhaps tasting the merest hint of salt from off his skin. He'd watch as her lips closed around his finger in a perfect 'O' as she sucked. Only softly at first, but then harder, making him breathe harshly, maybe even . . .

'Watch,' he said, and lifted his finger a little into the air in front of him — and firmly away from her.

She blinked, aware that she was the one breathing hard. She was the one caught in a web of sensuality. And then, the very next moment, before she had the chance to become angry or embarrassed, a flash of green and turquoise flashed across the air with a soft whirr of wings, and a small bird hovered over his finger.

Charmaine gasped. 'Oh. Oh, he's beautiful.'

'A sunbird, I think,' he said. 'Marissa, the owner of the café, has spent years teaching them this trick.'

The bird landed on Payne's finger and began to lick the jam with a long, sticky tongue.

'I can hardly feel him, he's so light,' Payne said, looking across at her, his heart contracting at the look of delighted wonderment in her eyes.

'Can I?' she wondered aloud, reaching for the spoon eagerly.

'Not too much,' he warned, and she put the merest speck of red onto her upturned fingertip.

The bird continued to feed hungrily on Payne's finger, but no other birds moved towards them. Then, just when she thought she would be out of luck, she caught a flash of crimson, black and white, out of the corner of her eye.

It was not a bird, however, but a butterfly, with elongated oval wings. She watched as it fluttered closer in that zigzagging haphazard flight unique to their species. Several times she thought it was going to fly away, but slowly it fluttered ever closer, seemed to hover playfully around her outstretched finger, as if working up the courage to land, then suddenly alighted.

Charmaine froze, determined not to scare the beautiful creature away. She was unaware how Payne stared at her, mesmerised by the sight. She looked so incredibly beautiful, rapt and blissful, in a world of her own.

And oh, he wanted her to look at him like that!

He shook his head, frightening the bird on his hand into sudden whirling flight.

If he had any sense, he'd find out what she was up to, teach her not to play games with him, then send her packing back to her Oxford cottage a much wiser and perhaps sadder woman.

That was what he should do.

But when she turned starry eyes back to him, he knew he'd never be able to do it.

Well, so be it.

He was going to have to have her now. Have to find out where this was all taking him. Because he was sure she had some sort of scheme in mind. And since scheming obviously didn't come naturally to her, he was intrigued to find out what was behind it all. And if a taunting little voice whispered at the back of his mind that he was well and truly snared, he ruthlessly pushed it aside. After all, he could handle a novice like this with one hand tied behind his back. Right?

Charmaine felt the words she'd been about to speak dry up in her throat. As if sensing her sudden panic, the butterfly flew away.

Why was he looking at her like that?

'Payne,' she croaked nervously.

'Yes?' he said harshly.

'Is something wrong?'

Payne smiled crookedly. 'Wrong? What could possibly be wrong?' And so saying, he reached forward and pulled her finger into his mouth.

She gasped as he sucked lustily on her digit, turning her breasts into twin peaks of desire and making her snatch her hand away as if she was being burned.

* * *

The sun was beginning to set as they drew up at a small private marina.

The bobbing yachts, furled sails gleaming white against the sea, their paintwork turning orange with the glow of the setting sun, moved up and down with the gentle swell of the sea.

'What are we doing here?' she asked, as he turned off the ignition and drew off his sunglasses.

'Dinner,' he said simply.

'Oh.' She was hardly dressed for dinner, but she wasn't about to point that out. Ever since that incredible moment in

69

the tea shop, she'd been aware that something had changed between them.

She wasn't sure what it was, but it made her even more nervous.

Oh, he'd been the perfect host ever since, showing off the island of which he was justly proud, and making sure she saw all the sights. But he seemed almost reserved. Wary. Watchful even.

Now she climbed out of the car and looked around nervously. She couldn't see a clubhouse.

Using one of the keys on his key ring, he unlocked the padlock securing the door in the chain-link fence, and she walked out onto the jetty. Through the gaps in the planks she could see the swirling motion of the sea beneath her.

'This way,' he lead her almost to the end, then turned, lightly climbing on board a large, sleek, ultra-modern yacht.

'I thought . . .' she began nervously, then bit her lip. What had she thought?

'Don't worry, I'm a good cook,' he called down. 'The crew always keep the fridge and pantry well stocked. I usually take her out at least once a week, but we'll dine in harbour tonight. It's the crew's night off.'

Charmaine looked up the gangplank at him, still hesitant.

'She belongs to you?' she asked finally, looking towards the prow and the name plate, where she read it aloud. '*Queen of Diamonds*.' She laughed softly. Who else could it possibly belong to?

'Come on up,' he said and disappeared inside. A moment later, lights softly gleamed from the interior.

She took a deep, deep breath and slowly made her way up the gangplank.

She'd never been on a yacht before in her life.

She stepped into a stateroom that, even to her untutored eyes, was the second word in luxury. Her feet sank down into thick carpet as she surveyed the enormous space, which housed dark brown leather sofas and smoky glass and chrome tables festooned with magazines, books and an impressive-looking hi-fi system.

Through an alcove she heard the sound of pots and pans, and slowly walked around. She was sure one of the oil paintings fastened onto the wall was by a famous French impressionist. An antiques drinks cabinet displayed an exquisite decanter and cut-glass tumbler set, as well as alcohol of every description. She sank down onto one of the sofas, only to get up and nervously prowl around again a moment later.

What was she doing here?

Doubtless the *Queen of Diamonds* had a master bedroom somewhere down below. Probably complete with a mirrored ceiling and black satin sheets!

OK, perhaps not, she admitted to herself a moment later. Not when she had evidence of such exquisite taste all around her.

But it would definitely have a bed. A big bed.

And a man like Payne Lacey would almost certainly expect to be joined in that bed later on.

He'd expect some return for all the time he'd lavished on her today, after all. Why, even now, he was neglecting his precious casino in order to wine and dine her. What happened when it came time to pay the piper?

'Pan-fried sea bass with a green salad all right?' he asked from just behind her, making her jump like a startled cat and shoot around.

'Oh, er, yes. Yes. Fine,' she stammered.

He returned to the kitchen, or galley, she supposed it should be called, and a moment later heard the sizzling of fish.

Nervously she pulled open some French doors and found herself out on deck, with the glorious panorama of a sunset over the ocean spread out in front of her in all its glory.

She should be happy.

She was exactly where she wanted to be. Her plan to snare and break Payne Lacey seemed well on track. She was young, about to dine with a rich and handsome suitor on his fabulous yacht, and she had all the delights of the Caribbean right there at her fingertips. So why did she feel so . . . miserable?

Because, she realised a moment later, it was all a sham. The man cooking her dinner was not her lover, but a man she despised. She was not here in pursuit of love, but for cold, meagre revenge.

Her life suddenly felt like nothing but a forgery, and her immediate future held nothing in store but a pile of comfortless ashes.

And it was then that it hit her, with all the force of a hammer blow. She was in love with Payne Lacey!

CHAPTER SEVEN

Charmaine clung weakly to the deck rail. In love? Now where had that preposterous notion come from? Of course she wasn't in love. Not with Payne Lacey, the man who wooed, threw over, and nearly killed her sister. She couldn't possibly be in love with him, of all men.

She shook her head, fighting off a giddying sense of panic. She was just . . . overwhelmed. Yes, that was all. After all, that was understandable, she told herself fervently.

As a child she'd always been shy, and in the shadow of her famous family and her beloved sister. So she'd sought refuge in her one talent, and through sheer hard work and diligence, had succeeded in the world of fashion design. But although her career had always been as bright and shining as anyone could have wished for, her social life had been non-existent. She had, literally, no experience of men. Even her closest male friend was gay.

So when a man like Payne Lacey suddenly began to court her, of course she was bowled over. She wouldn't be human otherwise. He was rich, sexy, handsome, exciting. All the things that were supposed to turn a girl's head.

But not her heart! There was nothing about the man that touched her heart — there couldn't be. He was callous, uncaring, and probably didn't even believe that such a thing as love actually existed. In his world, women were for wooing and bedding then dumping, ready for the next one.

She thought of his nephew and his defence of some unknown friend's wife and sighed. OK, so the man wasn't a total monster. No human being was. But that didn't mean she'd lost her heart to him. It didn't!

She inhaled deeply, relishing the perfume of night-blooming flowers scenting the sea breeze.

Perhaps she was just in love with this place, and with this moment in time. But not with the man. She couldn't be in love with the man. She wouldn't let herself be. It was just too . . . unthinkable.

'Dinner's ready,' he said softly, cutting across her agonised thoughts and making her whirl around with a small gasp. She had no idea how she looked in that moment, all bare-legged and defensive, eyes widened in alarm and lips softly parted.

For a second, his eyes seemed to glow as soft as a wisp of wood smoke. But surely that was an optical illusion she told herself unsteadily. There was nothing soft in this man's make-up!

And then he stepped aside, and she forced herself forward, back into the yacht's interior. She must act naturally. It was time she stopped being such a rabbit, she admonished herself, and showed some backbone.

He led her silently to the galley, which had its own dining room off to one side. As a centrepiece it had a small, round dark oak table and matching chairs. Pure white candles, held in intricate silver candlesticks, were placed either side of two perfectly laid-out table settings. A silver ice bucket contained an opened bottle of wine.

He pulled out the chair nearest to her, and she sank down gratefully, her heart fluttering in her breast.

The flicker of the candle glow cast her face into light and shadow, and rendered her silvery gold hair almost magical. When he reached out to pour the wine, his hand was not quite steady. He brought a huge wooden salad bowl to the table, then deftly slipped two perfectly fried pieces of fish onto the plates.

It looked and smelt wonderful, but Charmaine doubted her ability to force down a single bite.

'Is everything all right?' Payne said, sitting opposite her and opening out his napkin. The natural guttering of the candles was doing wonderful things to his dark gold hair and deeply bronzed skin, and she was almost sure she could feel the male strength oozing out of him with his every movement. She supposed working so hard in the gardens every day kept him super fit.

She wondered what it would feel like to slip her hand under his shirt and explore the washboard hardness of his abdomen and the firm muscles in his chest and biceps. What must it be like to touch a man that way?

She reached for her glass of wine and took a shaky sip. 'Of course, everything's fine. Just perfect,' she said, with a smile that felt as false as her words.

And suddenly, for the first time, it occurred to her what a mean thing she was planning to do. Lucy had got her heart broken by this man, but now that she'd actually met and had seen for herself his careless attitude to life, the insane risks he took, she would have bet her last penny that at least it hadn't been deliberate.

Lucy would have been fair game in his eyes — an up-and-coming actress, here for a holiday and perhaps a romance. It would never have even crossed his mind that she wouldn't know the rules. That she might actually fall in love. He would probably be amazed if she were to blurt out right now that her sister had been almost mortally wounded by his treatment of her.

So he was reprehensible, yes. But he was not deliberately cruel.

But she would have no such defence to put forward, should her own plan succeed, she realised miserably. She would have come here expressly to hurt and wound, humiliate and belittle. She'd have done it with her eyes wide open.

And as she stared at him across that candlelit table, she knew she couldn't do it.

Not now.

Payne too reached for his wine and sipped, but his eyes were shuttered and revealed nothing. Behind them, though, his mind was racing.

What was going on? She looked as if she'd just seen a ghost, or had lost her best friend, or had some other life-changing calamity befall her. What could he possibly have done or said to make her look like that?

'I'm really not very hungry, I'm afraid,' Charmaine said, picking up her fork, but only to listlessly part her fish and push the tender flakes around her plate.

'Not dieting I hope,' he said. 'You don't need to lose weight.'

Charmaine smiled. 'No, you needn't worry. Besides, Jonniee doesn't employ ultra-thin models.' She had always been horrified by the prospect of even unintentionally endorsing anorexia nervosa by going along with the trend for almost skeletal models, a policy in which Jo-Jo was in total accord. They both designed clothes for healthy women of all sizes.

Payne nodded. 'I'm pleased to hear it. You obviously run a good company,' he said, with deliberate emphasis on the word 'you'.

Charmaine nodded, and took another sip, apparently unaware of the implications in what he'd just said. Payne watched her closely, then saw her suddenly stiffen.

Charmaine looked at him with wide blue eyes, which had darkened in alarm. 'What do you mean? I don't run the company. Jo-Jo does.'

So she was still lying to him. Though it saddened and puzzled him, it somehow didn't surprise him. Payne leaned slowly back in his chair and swirled the wine in his glass. 'Don't you think it's time that that particular lie be allowed to die a graceful death, Charmaine?' he asked softly. 'I know you and Jo-Jo are full business partners, and that, creatively, you are the driving force behind one of the biggest and best fashion houses in the world. Tell me, are you ashamed of your designs? Or your partner? Or the company?'

'No, of course not! I love clothes, and stand by all my creations!' she said hotly. 'And Jo-Jo's marvellous at all sorts of things — promotions, getting orders from the big-name stores, doing the publicity and everything.'

She abruptly subsided as she realised, a little late, that she'd risen to the bait far too quickly. 'Anyway, how did you know?' she asked after a moment of tense silence.

Payne shrugged. 'Does it matter?'

Charmaine wasn't so sure. It depended on what else he knew. Did he know who her family was — who Lucy was? And if he did know, or regularly made it his business to know these sorts of things, how long would it be until he found out why she was really here?

It would be ironic if, just when she'd come to her senses and realised that she couldn't go through with her revenge, he found out about it and sent her packing.

The thought of never seeing him again was so painful it actually made her wince.

'So why all the secrecy?' Payne prodded softly, determined to get to the bottom of the mystery, and unwilling to let her off the hook now he had her on the run.

'It's no big deal. I just don't have that in-your-face personality that a fashion house needs to promote it,' Charmaine said, and gave what she hoped was an uncaring shrug.

'Unlike Jo-Jo,' Payne acknowledged with a grin. 'All right, I can see how your business partner earns his fifty percent, but what's wrong with your own contributions being acknowledged? Jo-Jo can still be the larger-than-life front man, while others are still made aware of your own input.'

'I don't like the limelight, I never have. That's for the rest of the family,' she said, then could have bitten off her tongue.

'Oh? They sound famous,' Payne said. So it was confirmed. He wondered who they could be. 'Entertainers of some kind, are they?'

Charmaine went pale. 'Only my father,' she lied, trying to gather her scattered wits. 'He's rather a name. On the stage. I don't want to talk about him,' she said, making it sound as if there was some big family rift. In reality, of course, nothing could be farther from the truth. Her father, Lucy and herself were actually very close.

'Look, it's getting late, I really must go,' she said, putting down her napkin with a shaking hand. Any moment now he was bound to think of Lucy, the nearly famous actress with a famous father. And then the game would be up.

But when she looked at him, he showed no signs of guessing her secrets. Instead, he looked bitterly disappointed.

And suddenly she knew why.

It was because she'd said she wanted to go, and he realised he would not have a bed-mate for the night after all. She almost wanted to laugh — except she felt like crying more.

'I have a shoot tomorrow,' she said, then wondered why she was trying to let him down lightly. Next she'd be anxiously trying to reassure him that he was a very sexy man, and of course she wanted him, any woman would.

But why should she, she thought defiantly. He was big enough and mean enough to take care of himself. And if he wasn't used to rejection — well, the change would do him good!

'But not until the afternoon,' he said, then raised an eyebrow as she looked at him askance. 'Jo-Jo told me the photographers would be all morning setting things up.'

Charmaine bit her lip. 'Even so, we models have to get our beauty sleep. Nobody wants a girl to show up with dark rings under her eyes.'

She glanced longingly at the door. Why wasn't he taking the hint? Would she really have to go out in search of a taxi? The marina had been far off the beaten track, and a mile or so from the nearest town. Still, she could walk it, if she had to, no problem. She took far longer walks in the countryside back home. Though it *was* getting dark . . .

'Yes, why are you suddenly modelling for your own fashion house, Charmaine?' he asked, and watched as all the colour drained from her face. 'I mean, a moment ago you were telling me you were the shy one in the family, but now — voila. You're reborn as a Jonniee model. You couldn't get to stand in more limelight than that if you tried.'

Charmaine gazed at him hopelessly. Why hadn't she seen that coming?

'I . . . I . . . er . . . I . . .' she swallowed and gulped, but no glib lie came to save her this time.

And slowly, Payne rose to his feet and came around the table. She pushed her chair back, glancing around wildly, the urge to flee sending her pulse rate rocketing.

'Let me guess,' he said softly, reaching for her and lifting her chin up tenderly with two fingers. He looked down searchingly into her lovely face, reading fear, pain and bewilderment in her eyes. 'You finally realised that life was passing you by, and knew you had to do something about it. That's it, isn't it?'

Charmaine blinked. What? 'Oh, y-yes,' she said. 'That's right. I needed a change.'

Payne's eyes narrowed for a moment. She was lying to him again. He just knew it. For a while there, he'd thought he was onto the truth at last. Unbelievably, this beautiful woman was shy and introverted, living a restricted and boring, loveless life. It had made sense to think that she'd come to her senses and realised she needed to break out of her shell. But that wasn't it, he knew that now. There was still something else. He was sure of it. She was up to something, or hiding something.

Well, two could play at games like that.

'Well,' he drawled, leaning closer, watching a tiny vein throb nervously at the base of her throat, 'I can help you with that. You want to live life to the full, Charmaine Reece, I'm your man. I'll show you the time of your life.'

And what, he wondered, fascinated, would she make of that?

Charmaine choked back a wild desire to laugh. She'd just bet he could. Oh yes. You wanted to dabble your toe in the world of male-female sexuality? Payne Lacey was an expert. You wanted to throw all caution to the wind and let chance or fate or sheer luck dictate your life — who better than a casino owner and noted gambler to lead the way? You wanted to get your heart broken and your life smashed to smithereens — call on an impresario.

'No thank you!' she snapped, standing abruptly and flushing wildly. 'Now, are you going to take me back to the hotel, or do I have to walk?'

Payne grinned. 'Oh, I think we can do better than that. There's a spare bedroom on board. More than one in fact.'

'If you think I'm going to spend the night on board this boat with you, then you have another think coming!' she all but shouted at him.

'What's the matter, little Charmaine? Scared?' he taunted. 'And I thought you were trying to be all grown up now.' He saw her hands clench into fists, and anticipated a stinging blow.

At least, if she were out of control, she might at last reveal her true self. He was sure, now more than ever, that she was covering something up, and doing herself no good in doing so. This woman was made for love and life and the good things. If only she'd let him give them to her!

Charmaine swallowed hard. Things were getting out of hand. She had to do something. Salvage something from this miserable mess.

'All right,' she said quietly. 'I have no sleeping things, no toothbrush even, but . . .' she tried to sound wearily resigned, like a grown-up indulging an aggravating child.

'We have all that in the guest bedroom,' Payne interrupted her ruthlessly, but his voice, in contrast, was soft and warm, almost apologetic. 'And it's all right. Really. Your sleep will be undisturbed, I promise.'

Charmaine smiled grimly. You bet it would be, she thought. Because I intend not only to lock my door, but also push a chair under the handle as well!

And as she allowed him to show her to her room — a lovely room in shades of peach and cream with turquoise accents — she was determined to remain cool and aloof at all times. No more acting like a screaming fishwife.

'The bathroom's just through there. Goodnight, sweetheart,' he said softly, and closed the door behind him.

He'd sounded so tender just then, so gentle, that for a moment she just stood there gaping at the closed door. Then she stopped daydreaming and turned the lock with a sharp, rewarding click, then reached for the nearest hardback chair and rammed it hard underneath.

But as she did so, she couldn't help but wonder. Was she really doing this to keep Payne Lacey out? Or to keep herself in? Because as she got ready for bed, then lay tossing and turning sleeplessly in the big queen-sized bed, her body ached for something far more alluring than sleep. And she knew that, if she didn't keep herself rigidly lying in the bed, then no locked door or cleverly placed chair would keep her from making an utter fool of herself.

* * *

When she awoke, she was puzzled. Something was very strange. And then she realised what it was. She was moving. Or rather, the whole room was moving!

It took her a moment to remember the events of last night, and then she shot up in bed and glanced wildly around. But the chair was still in place and she hadn't gone sleepwalking in the night.

Another glance at her watch showed her it was nearly eleven o'clock in the morning! With a small cry she shot up and went to the shower, washing her hair and changing back into her shorts and T-shirt. What she really wanted to put on was something white and floating. But what was the use of making herself look good for Payne? It was not as if she could ever allow him to actually be her lover.

She sighed and stepped back out on deck, surprised to see that they were nearly at Gold Rock Beach, near the Palace and her own small hotel. In fact, a few minutes later the engines stopped and she heard the unfamiliar clanking of chains as the anchor was lowered.

'Hello, sleepy head,' Payne said cheerfully, suddenly appearing beside her. 'Do you want breakfast — or should I say brunch, or are you anxious to get back to the hotel?'

'The hotel, I think,' she said quickly, refusing to meet his eyes.

She watched him climb lightly down a ladder on the side of the yacht and release a small boat with a foldaway outboard motor. Once he was on safely on board, she turned around and backed carefully down the ladder herself, knowing all the while that he was looking up at her, and her nearly exposed bottom in the tight-fitting shorts.

She stepped onto the boat, which rocked treacherously beneath her, and sat down on a wooden plank seat a little more quickly and far more firmly than she'd intended. She shot him a look, just daring him to speak, but he was looking innocently behind him, fiddling with a rope.

When he turned back to her, his face was utterly deadpan. 'Ready?' he asked.

She nodded, her lips pressed tight in a thin, hard line.

As they neared the beach, it became apparent that the arrival of the luxury yacht hadn't gone unnoticed. On the beach, first Jo-Jo, then Phil, then the rest of the models became clearly visible.

And her heart sank.

They all came forward, chattering like excited magpies, as Payne expertly beached the craft, while Charmaine was clambering out almost before it had stopped.

'Wow, what a boat,' Dee-Dee said, shading her eyes as she looked towards the *Queen of Diamonds*. 'Is it yours?'

'Of course it's his,' Jo-Jo said, then sighed wistfully. 'No chance of doing a shoot on board, I suppose,' he asked cheekily.

'No chance at all,' Payne grinned back.

Charmaine suddenly became aware of a pair of eyes boring into her back, and turned to see Jinx glaring at her. She was topless, and had obviously been deepening her tan in preparation for the afternoon's shoot. She looked stunning. And nobody was noticing her. No wonder she looked ready to spit fire.

Charmaine looked hastily away, and caught Jo-Jo's eye. 'I'm not late for the shoot am I?' she asked guiltily.

'No, no, that's fine,' her friend said, looking from her to the yacht, then to Payne and back to her. Then his eyes scanned her casual clothes knowingly, and he smiled.

Charmaine flushed, realising at once that Jo-Jo must have seen her leave yesterday in this outfit and had, correctly if erroneously, assumed that they'd spent the night together. And so had Jinx, if the waves of fulminating pique and anger coming off her were anything to go by.

'In fact, Phil has found two locations, and we're shooting Coral and Jinx there this afternoon, but the rest of you somewhere else tomorrow morning. Very early, to get the sunrise. So you can have the rest of the day off.'

'Yes, darling, and if you take my advice, you'll spend it sleeping,' Jinx said, and added spitefully, 'Someone really should have told you that it's just so unprofessional to come in looking like you haven't slept a wink. Even when you haven't.'

Even Dee-Dee shot Jinx a surprised look at that. Jo-Jo stiffened but before he could reprimand her, Payne reached out for Charmaine's hand, not surprised to find it as cold as ice.

'Seeing as you have the rest of the day off,' he said loudly, 'why don't you come back onto the boat. A queen deserves the presence of another queen, don't you think?'

The name of the boat was plainly visible out in the bay, and Charmaine felt her heart melt at his surprising and very public defence of her.

'All right,' she said, knowing she was a fool to let Jinx's bile force her into even closer proximity to Payne, but she wouldn't have been human if she hadn't felt a thrill of triumph at the sick look that crossed the red-headed model's face.

Payne was telling everyone, in effect, that she was his girl, and so watch out. It was heady stuff, and she had to keep reminding herself that it wasn't true. He was just being kind, knowing how much Jinx's cruel words could wound her.

As she hurried back to the hotel, changed her underwear, and then stood indecisively in front of the mirror, Charmaine was aware that she was feeling something she'd never really felt before.

What was it exactly? Thrilled. Charmed. Yes, all of that. And why not — a man like Payne had chosen her over someone like Jinx. He wanted her. Wanted to spend time with her.

And she . . .

Her hand, hovering over a white silk dress with a floating hemline and pretty cross-strapped neckline, hesitated.

Yes, exactly what was she doing?

Hadn't she just decided that she no longer planned to get her revenge on Payne? And hadn't last night shown her she was playing way out of her league?

So what was she doing now?

She didn't know. She was out of control. Her hands had taken the dress from the hanger and were pulling it over her head before she knew what she was about.

It was as if her body knew what it was doing, even if her mind and soul didn't.

She added a pale pink lipstick to her mouth and slipped on a pair of flat but delicate white sandals. She brushed out her hair vigorously, then forced herself to meet her own reflection in the mirror.

Had she gone mad? It seemed the only explanation.

But as she met the bright, intense sparkle in her blue eyes, she realised something else. She might well be mad, but she also felt alive.

Truly, zestfully, wonderfully alive.

And Payne Lacey was the reason why.

CHAPTER EIGHT

Charmaine hastily thrust a peach-coloured bikini, a large beach towel, a bottle of sun-tan lotion, a pair of sunglasses and a pair of flip flops into a bag and raced out of the door.

She almost expected him to be gone, like a promised Christmas present that never materialised come the big day, but no, he was still on the beach, leaning against the tender, his long legs thrust forward, feet almost buried in the sand. He was wearing a white T-shirt that hugged the contours of his upper torso, and a light sea breeze ruffled his dark gold hair.

His eyes lit up as he saw her coming across the beach towards him, and Charmaine felt her heart stutter, like a faulty engine. He was glad to see her. Really glad. For the first time in her life, a man desired her and wanted to spend his time with her, and the knowledge was so heady she felt almost drunk with it.

She sounded as breathless as she felt as she slung her bulging bag into the small boat. 'All set. Has Jo-Jo gone?' She looked around, but the models and the rest of the gang were nowhere to be seen.

'They all trundled off to get some shots in Lucayan,' Payne faithfully repeated Jo-Jo's message. 'You're not to worry, but enjoy yourself for the rest of the day.'

Charmaine glanced at him, one eyebrow lifted. 'Oh yes? His orders, or yours?' she teased. She didn't need to be a genius to understand where all this sudden self-confidence had come from. She felt as if she could take on the world, so long as Payne's eyes always lit up like that whenever she was near.

Payne grinned widely. 'Both. Now, how do you fancy snorkelling?'

* * *

She fancied snorkelling very well, as it turned out. After returning them to the *Queen of Diamonds* he took the yacht around to the other side of the island, where 'a nice little shipwreck' had been attracting sea life for the last decade or so. It was, he assured her, in relatively shallow waters, and luckily they had the popular site to themselves as he weighed anchor.

'You can swim, right?' Payne asked, letting a pair of snorkels and masks fall onto the deck, then watching her appreciatively as she bent down to examine the gear more closely.

She was wearing the beach towel draped, sarong-wise, around her, for when he'd gone below to change, she'd suddenly felt overwhelmed with that old familiar enemy, shyness. Perhaps it was because the bikini made her feel worse than naked — if there was such a thing! Perhaps it was because she was slowly becoming aware of how isolated they were out here on his boat, with nobody for miles around.

Or yet again, perhaps it was simply because she could feel something in the air, a portent that some life-altering event was about to happen to her. Whatever it was, she was glad to be able to push all these thoughts to the back of her mind and think and speak about something as mundane as swimming instead.

'Of course I can swim,' she said now, then was forced to add honestly, 'though probably not very well.'

'OK, well there's nothing to worry about,' he reassured her. 'I'll be right beside you every moment. And we always have these,' he added, opening a locker on the deck and producing some inflatable water-wings.

Again her amused laughter tinkled across the deck, making him wish that she would laugh more often. It suited her.

'Oh, I think I can manage without those,' she demurred, then began to listen in earnest as he explained the principles of snorkelling, and the safety measures needed. Next he gave a practical demonstration of how to prevent the face mask from misting up and how to use the snorkel itself.

'Remember, try not to bite down,' he finished. 'I know it's a natural reaction, but try to resist it.'

Charmaine nodded seriously. But biting down on her snorkel was not the only thing she was trying to resist! She also very much wanted to lean across, take the contraption from his mouth, and kiss him until he begged for mercy, and this temptation was giving her far more trouble than a simple piece of rubber!

To take his concentration off the lesson and return it firmly to her was a need so strong that it was actually making her shake. She wanted to make him notice that she was more or less naked underneath this towel, and once he did, she just knew . . .

'Right then, ready?'

Charmaine blinked. 'Er, yes. Ready.'

'And you remember the signals?'

Signals? What signals? She really had been daydreaming when she should have been paying attention.

Payne's eyes glittered as if aware of her bewilderment, and she flushed as she wondered if he could read her mind and know what had caused her distraction.

'Yes. Signals,' he reiterated firmly. 'The thumb and finger together in an O, the universal sign for everything being OK, and the flat hand, waved up and down, for a problem.'

'Oh yes. Right,' she said, standing upright again, and trying to tell herself it was only the slight rocking motion of the ship that was making her feel so giddy.

Then her mouth went dry as he stood up and pulled the T-shirt off his torso, revealing deeply bronzed skin and a powerful chest. It really wasn't fair for a man to be so beautiful. What sculptor or painter wouldn't want to capture his physique in marble or oils?

He dipped suddenly, and she realised he was pulling off his shorts! Her lungs exhaled all the air from them as if she'd just been punched. Surely he wasn't going to swim naked!

No, she realised in bitter disappointment a moment later, he wasn't. Underneath he wore a pair of black swimming trunks that did very little to conceal the hard male dominance of his loins. His tanned thighs, like moulded iron, clenched and moved with fluid ease as he knelt on one knee to pick up the gear.

Suddenly, he lifted his head sharply to look up at her, as if some male instinct suddenly alerted him to danger. Or to something even more potent and powerful.

Their eyes clashed, clung and seemed to speak without the clumsy need for words.

And Charmaine experienced one of those moments that would remain with her forever.

With him knelt before her like this, almost naked, as if a slave in front of his queen, she felt suddenly aflame. Conflicting emotions bombarded her from all directions. She wanted so much, so many different things, and she wanted them all right now. This instant.

She wanted him to kiss her feet, to run his tongue around her ankles, then up her shin, around her calf, moving up to lick the small indent at the back of her knee.

She wanted to reach down and pull him up to face her, so that she would be free of this tormenting moment.

She wanted to bend down and push him back onto the deck, rip those black swimming trunks off him and make love to him as no other woman ever had before or could again.

She wanted him to pretend that none of this was happening so that she could pretend the same.

She wanted him not to be looking at her with those ocean-deep grey eyes. And yet she wanted him to keep looking at her like that forever.

She shook her head helplessly. And as if in answer to her unspoken appeal for help, slowly, and holding her eyes with his own all the time, Payne rose to his feet and towered over her. The air around them became charged with electricity, as if a sudden hurricane had emerged and was threatening to blow them both away.

His voice, when he spoke, was husky with desire. 'Take that towel off,' he rasped, but even before she had a chance to register his words, let alone obey, he was reaching out and yanking it away.

She took a tiny step forward to keep her balance, and shivered at her sudden exposure. She tensed a little as he dropped his eyes to look down at her, then relaxed as she saw the desire in them intensify and burn.

'You're so beautiful,' he said, almost in accusation. She tensed as he lifted his hand, and then sighed as he ran one finger lightly down the side of her neck, over her shoulder and down one arm. Her skin tingled wherever his finger-tip touched, and her knees began to tremble warningly. She could feel her breasts swell, the tender nipples pushing hard and urgently against the material of her bikini, begging for the loving attention of his tongue.

'You know I want you, don't you?' he challenged gruffly, and Charmaine didn't need to look down to where his man-hood was straining hard against his swimming trunks in order to nod agreement.

'And you want me?' he persisted.

Charmaine licked her lips, aware of a faint taste of salt on them. She lifted her head and met his grey gaze head on.

'Yes,' she said sadly. 'But it's not a good idea.'

She'd spoken the literal truth. She was, in that moment of self-revelation, unable to lie or prevaricate. She did want him. But it was such a bad idea. At least, for her it was. Not only was she becoming increasingly concerned about the safety of her own heart, but what about her sister? Just how far had she intended to take things to avenge Lucy? If she wasn't careful she could end up doing more harm than good here.

'Let's go snorkelling then, shall we?' she gritted, stepping back and walking to the rail. Although she'd never dived in her life, she was so desperate to get off that boat and away from his potent charm that she clambered over the rails and did a less than graceful belly flop into the sea.

What she really needed was for it to be stone cold and grimly uninviting. Something to shock her back to sanity. Instead she sank beneath crystal clear warm blue water and emerged a moment later, her body still singing for his touch, her mind still crying out for what it had lost. And must never have.

On the deck, Payne looked down at her. His hands were clenched into fists and he looked thunderously angry.

What the hell was she playing at? Leading him one moment, then just turning things off the next, as if he was some sort of tap. What did she think — that what had just happened had no more meaning than turning down the offer of a drink?

There was a word for women like her. A nasty word. And it was a word, he slowly began to realise, that simply didn't apply to her. As he forced himself to ignore the clamouring heat and urgent demands of his body, his mind played back the last few minutes.

He had always trusted his instincts — always. They were what made him such a devastatingly good poker player, and had been largely responsible for his incredible luck. And his instincts told him that this girl really was an innocent abroad. In spite of her incredible beauty, he was sure her lack of guile was genuine. Jinx's cruel words this morning had penetrated a delicate skin, not a hard hide grown callous over the years. So she was no femme fatale playing dangerous games. He would bet his life on that.

So, if she wasn't playing an elaborate teasing game, what had just happened?

As he leant on the rail and watched her do an inexpert breaststroke away from the yacht, he tried to clear his mind and concentrate.

It still wasn't easy. She had him tied up in knots! Not surprising, since the sexual chemistry had been there, right from the start. She'd certainly come on board his boat today willingly. In fact, he'd sensed a hidden, almost defiant excitement in her ever since she'd returned with her bag full of beach gear. So it wasn't as if he was mistaking the signals.

And that breathtaking moment when he'd looked up at her from the deck had been more than reciprocal. She'd wanted him as much as he'd wanted her. She'd even admitted as much.

Then something had changed. The moment, the passion, the connection had somehow vanished.

'Why isn't it a good idea, Charmaine?' he called down softly, but she was too far away to hear him.

Quickly he reached for the gear and did a straight and clean feet-first dive into the sea, popping up like a cork a moment later and swimming in an easy, energy-efficient overarm crawl towards her.

'The wreck's just over there,' he said, careful to keep his voice matter-of-fact, and pointing to where a bright orange buoy, marking the place as a possible navigational hazard, bobbed at the surface.

'OK,' she said, with forced cheerfulness, and set off in her hesitant breaststroke. Silently, he kept pace beside her. If she wanted to pretend that nothing had happened, well, then, he was more than willing to play along.

Her hair had darkened a shade in the water, and through the tint of aquamarine, her limbs looked paler than usual. He swallowed back yet another surge of desire, and while she clung to the buoy to get her breath back he stayed nearby, treading water, but keeping a discreet distance.

Charmaine shot him a glance out of the side of her eye. What was he thinking? Was he still angry?

While she'd been waiting for him to join her in the sea, she'd had a chance to start feeling guilty. Oh, she knew she had a right to self-defence, and not letting Payne Lacey break her heart was a legitimate (if unofficial) human right, but she really shouldn't have let things go so far.

'Ready?' he asked at last, and handed over a face mask and snorkel.

She nodded, slipped them on a little awkwardly, then began to swim, face down, feeling uneasy now that she couldn't see him.

But then the magic and the beauty of what lay revealed beneath her gradually began to filter through her misery.

The wreck was of an old fishing trawler, colonised now by beautiful, coloured coral in tones of pink, orange, yellow and white. And swimming in and out of them were vibrantly coloured fish and shrimp, the likes of which she had only seen before on wildlife documentaries on the television.

Out of the corner of her eye she kept catching glimpses of Payne — his arms or legs cutting smoothly through the water, always near but never obstructing her view, making her feel safe. Water was not her natural element, and she had nothing like his expertise or familiarity with the sea, but if anything were to happen, she just knew she'd be all right as long as Payne was there.

Funny. She could trust a man with her life, but not her body, or her heart. Or her future.

No, on second thoughts, she corrected herself, as her eyes misted over with unshed tears, concealing her view of the fabulous, man-made reef, there was nothing funny about it at all.

She lifted her head, and spat the snorkel out of her mouth, and determinedly swallowed back her tears. She surreptitiously wiped her eyes as she felt Payne bob up beside her.

'Everything all right?' he asked.

'Yes, fine,' she lied, forcing a bright smile onto her face, which felt as artificial as Formica. 'I just needed to clear my mask.'

By now she'd forced the tears back inside, and re-donning the mask, she looked down once more.

And almost screamed. Except of course, you couldn't scream with a snorkel in your mouth.

She jerked upright, splashing and nearly slipping under.

'Hey, careful,' Payne said sharply, catching her arm and lifting her chin above water. 'What's wrong?' he snapped as he took in the sudden pallor of her face and the panic in her lovely eyes.

'Sh-shark,' she managed to jerk out. Was it even now powering towards them, its cold fish eyes and even colder fish heart centred on their thrashing legs? Without a word, Payne bobbed down, making her scream his name in panic.

'Payne NO!'

He'd be killed. And the thought of never seeing him again filled her with morbid dread. Any thought for her own safety or mortality faded into insignificance. Besides, what did it matter if she died too? She wouldn't want to go on living without him anyway.

She almost sobbed with relief as his blond head, slick with sea water, popped back up.

For a second she could hardly believe her eyes. He was grinning — actually laughing. What was wrong with this man? Did he have so little fear of death or danger that he literally laughed in the face of it?

'It's a tiddler,' he crowed. 'And a completely harmless species anyway.' Then all laughter fled as he realised the extent of her horror. 'Oh, sweetheart, you didn't think I'd have brought you out here if it was dangerous did you?' he said with concern, propelling himself towards her and grabbing hold of her firmly. 'Darling, I promise you, we're perfectly safe. I wouldn't let anything hurt you, I swear.'

And he meant it.

Charmaine nodded, knowing that he spoke the truth, and knowing too that he was waiting for her to speak, to say that she was OK, maybe even to laugh it all off.

It was just a silly scare, that was all. The kind of thing you'd look back on later and feel ashamed of for being so frightened. She knew all that, but still she didn't speak. She couldn't. But not because of the shark. It was because she was still reeling from the impact of that moment when she thought he was going to die.

She'd been devastated. In fact, she'd almost felt as if she herself was dead already.

And that intensity could only mean one thing.

She hadn't been mistaken.

She really was in love with Payne Lacey.

* * *

The next half an hour passed in a blur. She was vaguely aware of him urging her back to the boat, of climbing the ladder while he swarmed up behind her, hovering over her and all but hauling her up the rungs himself. She barely acknowledged the warm blanket he slipped around her shoulders, and she sipped out of the balloon glass of brandy he pressed on her without even tasting the fiery liquid that gradually warmed and thawed her.

She was dimly aware that he was trying to reassure her about the shark and apologising all the time for her fright. In some still-functioning part of her mind, she even knew that he must be silently berating himself for bringing her snorkelling.

And she wanted to reassure him that that wasn't it. The shark didn't matter. But if she did that, then she'd have to come up with some other reason for her shock.

And she could hardly blurt out the real reason for that, could she?

How embarrassing it would be for him. What a nuisance to have a smitten woman around. She was supposed to be a sophisticated model, a seen-it-all, done-it-all woman of the world who knew the rules. Jinx would never do something so crass as to fall in love with a man who only wanted a few weeks' dalliance in the sun.

And so she let him tuck her feet underneath her on the sofa, and closed her eyes and pretended to sleep. And tried not to think about what would happen next. Because, now more than ever, that vision of her lonely future looked totally inescapable.

* * *

Payne watched her sleeping and cursed himself silently. Of all the stupid things to do. He should have warned her about the small sharks. They were harmless enough, but he should have known that just their presence would be enough to scare her. She was not a native, after all, she wasn't used to such things.

He was a fool. All kinds of a fool.

He groaned as he remembered the horror in her eyes as she stared at him, out there in the water. She'd looked as if her world was coming to an end. But she must have known that even if it had been a Great White down there, he'd have killed it before he let it get anywhere near her. Women just knew these things. They knew when they had a man hopelessly hooked.

And he was hooked, he finally admitted to himself.

It was a thought far more frightening than any shark! And yet, as he gazed down at the sleeping beauty on his sofa, he just wished he could make her understand that he'd do anything to keep her safe. He'd do anything to make her happy.

Anything at all.

He sighed and leaned back on the chair, closing his eyes. As he did so, Charmaine risked peeking out from under her lashes, saw that he wasn't looking her way, and watched him openly.

He really was breathtaking. His hair had dried in clumps, still sticky from the sea, and she yearned to smooth it down with her fingers. She knew it would be so easy to get up and go to him, perhaps slip onto his lap and startle him awake. Then she could kiss him, long and lovingly, not even trying to hide her emotion for him, and then let him carry her into the bedroom. He was welcome to her virginity. He was welcome to all she possessed.

It would be worth all the heartache that would follow, she just knew it would. It would be bliss. And, after all, she might never fall in love again. Oh yes, it would be so easy to convince herself that it was better to love and lose than never love at all. And that being Payne Lacey's lover was worth any pain or consequence. And if it was only herself that she had to think of, she knew she'd be making love to him right now.

But there was Lucy.

How could she betray Lucy by taking up with the man she had loved so much that she'd almost killed herself because of him? How could she add a second betrayal to the one she'd already suffered? How could her own sister stab her in the back like that?

The stark, unalterable, unbearable answer to that was simple.

She couldn't.

CHAPTER NINE

Charmaine watched Jinx slip back out through Payne's office door and slink away like a cat that had not only had the cream, but the odd canary or two as well.

She bit her lip and tried to concentrate on what Coral was saying, but found it almost impossible. They were doing the final shots inside the casino, and she was wearing a shimmering bronze silk creation that worked wonders with the red lighting Phil had set up.

But her mind was far from work.

What had Jinx been up to in the office with Payne? True, she'd gone in there without an invitation, that much she'd been able to see for herself, but he'd hardly thrown her out within ten seconds flat, had he?

'Fizz, you're up next,' the photographer called, and Charmaine sank back into one of the few armchairs scattered about the casino's main gambling room, her eyes straying broodingly to the closed office door again and again. What had they talked about in there? Why had Jinx looked so pleased with herself?

Had Payne got bored with her already? And if so, who could blame him? From his point of view, she blew hot and cold, one minute egging him on, the next pushing him away, and who needed that in their lives?

Time dragged.

It had seemed to drag ever since that awful afternoon on his yacht. She'd been pathetic! Crying like a baby, just because she couldn't have something she wanted. It was shameful. Except that she knew, deep down inside, that it wasn't, not really. Because she wasn't being denied a new car, or a flash holiday, or the latest in designer earrings. She was being denied the man she loved, and her heart was breaking because of it. And if you couldn't cry over something like that, what could you cry over?

There was no way around it — she was in a world of hurt, and trying to pretend it was all some minor inconvenience that she'd grow out of one day was not helping one little bit.

Neither was Payne's attitude towards her. Ever since they'd got back from that ill-fated afternoon's snorkelling, he'd been aloof and distant. Oh, not obviously so — he still paid her attention, and looked the epitome of the attentive boyfriend. But she knew differently. She could see it in his eyes. He was holding back, playing a role, probably as a prelude to letting her down gently. And why not? He probably still thought that she'd had a fit of the vapours over one little harmless shark, and in this day and age, what man wanted a shrinking violet for a partner?

Certainly not a man like Payne. A man who bet hotels on a turn of the card! He'd want a woman as wild and free-spirited as himself, not some damp squib of an English rose.

And she couldn't tell him differently, that was what was so frustrating. To be in love with someone who didn't love you was one thing. To be in love with someone you knew you couldn't and mustn't have was yet another. But to be in love with someone who thought you were wet and pathetic was something else altogether!

She bit her lip to prevent more tears of self-pity forming in her eyes, and forced herself to concentrate on the photoshoot. The stunning black model who was draped across an art-deco bar and sipping an outrageous cocktail was wearing one of Jo-Jo's designs in beige suede. She was flirting with Phil's camera as if it were the man of her dreams. Charmaine was sure that Fizz would never disappoint a man.

Oh stop it, she told herself morosely. She would just have to lump it. Other women got over broken hearts and lived to tell the tale. She would do the same.

Just then the door to his office opened and Payne walked out, and she caught her breath painfully. He was wearing a black tuxedo and red bow tie, and looked stunning.

Of course, this was the night when friends and invited guests were going to join the shoot as background 'extras'. She supposed it amused the island's great and good to be an accessory in a glossy photoshoot. It was probably all part and parcel of their glamorous lifestyles — dinner in Paris, Royal Ascot, the film festival at Cannes, oh yes — and helping out their good friend Payne, by being photographed in his casino by a famous fashion house.

Some had already arrived and were sipping cocktails at the bar further along, the men eyeing her openly, while their women appraised her gown with envy.

It all felt so empty. So pointless.

She saw Payne scan the room, his eyes finding hers and lingering for just a wonderful, wonderful moment, then moving on. She let out a long, harsh breath, and wished she didn't have the whole evening still to get through.

Half an hour later, Payne was still mingling with his friends and guests when Phil called her name.

She was aware of being the centre of interest now, and forced her bare shoulders back and put a sway into her walk. After all, she was putting on a show, nothing more. Nobody in this room, with the exception of Jo-Jo, probably even thought of her as a person. To the men, she was just a beautiful model — someone to brag about meeting perhaps, over a dinner at the club. To the women, she was merely a clothes horse, someone to show how the gown she was wearing might look on themselves.

Her hair was done up in a complicated top knot, allowing platinum tendrils to curl down past her ears, her neck, and rest lightly on one shoulder. With the gown she wore simple beaten copper earrings and nothing else. The dress was very much the star.

'All right, I think we'll have you by the backgammon table,' Phil said, thinking immediately that Charmaine was oozing class, and backgammon was the game most people associated with the upper crust. She certainly looked as if she could be married to some earl or playboy prince.

'Now, I want you to look off a little to your left and look wistful,' Phil instructed and Charmaine nodded, doing as she was told. And found herself looking straight at Payne, who was sandwiched between an obvious husband-and-wife couple who were both talking to him at once. What was worse, he was obviously talking about her, but in that throwaway, off-hand kind of way that you talked about mere acquaintances.

If he was trying to make it clear to her that he was distancing himself from her, he couldn't have done a better job if he'd taken out an ad.

'Great, wonderful,' Phil enthused, snapping away. 'Now, I want you to look amused, as if something entertaining is happening just in front of you.'

Charmaine couldn't help but smile at that. Something entertaining was happening right in front of her, she thought helplessly. If you counted watching your whole world crumble as such.

'Fine, fine. A little more aggro now. As if you want to hit out.'

And so it went on. Finally she was allowed to go, and Dee-Dee took over. She began to make her way towards the dressing room, although there was no hurry to change, when suddenly the wife of the couple called her over.

'Hello there, coo-eee,' she called loudly, in an unmistakable Australian accent. 'Do you want a drink, chuck?' she asked, deftly relieving a waiter of a glass of champagne as she did so.

Charmaine could hardly turn her back and walk away, could she? But she felt her feet dragging as they carried her over to where Payne watched her approach with hooded eyes.

'Madge, Timmo, this is Charmaine Reece, the designer for Jonniee,' he introduced her not as a model but under her real auspices, and she shot him a quick, angry look.

'How do you do,' Charmaine said politely, shaking hands with the couple. Timmo had the look of a farmer, not too tall but wiry, and burnt the colour of a hazelnut. She could well imagine him owning vast areas of the Australian outback. Both of them had that warm and open-hearted attitude so particular of the Australians.

'Here, try this,' Madge said, handing over the glass. 'Bubbly always picks me right up. I reckon getting your picture taken like that takes more out of you than people might think.'

Charmaine smiled and gratefully took the glass. She was feeling thirsty, and drained.

'Hello, here's Max,' Timmo said, and they all turned to watch a tall, dark-haired man come across the crowded room to meet them.

'Hello, everyone,' the newcomer said amiably, and instantly Charmaine recognised his voice. This was the man who'd been talking to Payne in the garden that day. The one Payne had been angry with.

Charmaine's eyes sharpened on him in curiosity. He was a good-looking man, a few years older than Payne, and probably in some lucrative business such as antiques or wine growing. He had that look about him.

'Max, you look done in, sweetheart,' Madge said tactlessly, but the other man merely shrugged.

'Combination of jetlag and depression,' he said surprisingly, but with a self-mocking smile.

'Oh, trouble?' Madge said, instantly and unashamedly curious, and Payne grimaced openly.

'Trust you,' Timmo said to his wife, but everyone else smiled, and it was obvious to Charmaine that these were all old and trusted friends, and that nobody took Madge's larger-than-life personality to heart.

'Actually yes,' Max said ruefully. 'And since it'll be all over the island before long, I suppose you might as well be the first to know, Madge. Maria and I are splitting up.'

'Oh, darlin', that's a blow,' Madge said, instantly sympathetic.

'It's been coming for some time,' Max said philosophically, but not without regret, and Charmaine tried to sidle away. This was obviously not the kind of conversation meant for strangers.

'Payne, I was wondering if you knew a good divorce lawyer,' she heard Max say, as she mumbled something vague about needing to get into her next outfit.

'And before you lay into me, it's not for me, but for Maria,' Max added, while Madge gave her a small wave goodbye, before turning back to far more interesting goings-on. 'I want her to have the best. I don't want any hard feelings.'

Charmaine wondered if that's how all divorces were nowadays. It sounded wonderfully civilised, but she still felt sad as she walked back to the small office that was the dressing room and got into her next outfit. Even though she didn't know the couple involved, the failure of a marriage had to be something that left the world a little worse off than before.

Jinx was leaning across a desk, examining her make-up in the mirror, and Charmaine felt her spirits droop even lower. But luckily, just then Fizz came in, having finished her second stint, and immediately began regaling Jinx with the tale of her latest lover — a French count, who was married and refusing to leave his wife and three children.

This is definitely not the kind of life for me, Charmaine thought, trying not to feel shocked as she slipped the fabulous bronze gown over her head and slipped into a slinky

103

black beaded cocktail dress, her final outfit of the shoot. She was just not cut out for the hardness of it all. Perhaps a small country cottage and Wordsworth were all she was fit for.

When she went back into the main salon, Max's prediction that his news would soon be all over town was proving true, because already she could overhear people talking about it.

'I heard he was seeing some other woman,' a formidable-looking society dowager, dripping diamonds and malice, whispered loudly to another, slightly younger and more blasé woman.

'An actress, I heard,' she murmured vaguely. 'They usually are, aren't they? Or models.'

And suddenly Charmaine realised they'd both broken off their conversation to look at her! Blushing scarlet, she hurried away, her head down, and feeling — foolishly — ashamed.

Yes, there was no doubt about it, she couldn't wait to get away from this place. It had brought her nothing but misery and heartache.

But as she took her place next to Coral and waited for her turn with Phil, she found her eyes seeking out one man. And she knew that in spite of everything, and even given the whole wide world to choose from, there was no other place she'd rather be than right here, right now.

Because this was where Payne was.

* * *

It was nearly midnight by the time the photoshoot finally ended, and she was the first one away, slipping out into the gardens with relief. She guessed the 'wrap' party would go on until well into the early hours, but she was exhausted.

She made her way back to the hotel, the lobby of which was deserted at that hour, and went up to her room.

She had just slipped off her shoes, taken down her hair and wiped off her make-up when there was a tap at her door.

She paused in front of the mirror, a cotton-wool pad in one hand, a bottle of cleanser in the other.

Who on earth? She put the things down and walked to the door and tentatively opened it.

'Payne!' she gasped, opening the door wider before she considered the consequences. 'What are you doing here?' she blurted.

'Sorry but you left this behind,' he said, handing over her bag.

'Oh, thanks,' she said blankly. He could always have handed it in downstairs, or waited until the morning, couldn't he?

'Er, come in. I was just about to have some coffee,' she lied. 'Would you like a cup?'

'I'd love to. It's been one hell of a night,' he said wryly, coming in and looking around the small but pretty room with interest.

Charmaine, more nervous than she could ever remember being in the whole of her life, plugged in the kettle and reached for one of the sachets of coffee that the hotel provided. 'Milk, sugar?'

'Black's fine,' he said, his eyes going to the bed, and smiling at the sight of her plain white nightshirt. No sexy teddy for Charmaine.

He prowled the room, coming to a halt at the dressing table and the photograph in pride of place upon it. It was a picture of two women, faces pressed together, both laughing at the camera. Charmaine was unmistakable of course, her face make-up free, big blue eyes like Ceylon sapphires sparkling out at him.

And he recognised the other woman instantly too.

Lucy.

His eyes narrowed. His hand, which had been in the act of reaching out to bring the photograph closer, suddenly froze in mid-air.

Was Lucy part of her famous family? Well, why not? Now he came to think of it, he could remember Lucy talking about having an older sister. And he'd instantly recognised the name of the venerable doyen of the British stage and screen when Lucy had talked about her father.

So Charmaine was the other daughter. The one who didn't like the limelight.

Things were beginning to make sense at last.

He turned abruptly as he sensed Charmaine coming towards him with two coffee mugs, and he quickly moved away from the table.

'Thanks,' he headed towards the French windows and stepped out onto the modest balcony and Charmaine, after a moment's hesitation, stepped out to join him.

'Are the nights always this lovely?' she asked wistfully, looking up at a velvety sky, the stars bright as diamonds, while a half-moon silvered the Caribbean Sea as it lapped against the white sandy beach just yards away.

'Yes, usually,' Payne said quietly. 'You've fallen in love with the place too then?'

Charmaine caught her breath. 'Yes,' she husked. 'Yes, I've fallen in love with the Bahamas.'

And you. Oh, and you.

She turned abruptly and leant on the rail, looking out over the sea, turning her face from him, lest he read the truth in her eyes. Even in the moonlight, she was afraid that he'd be able to see right through her.

'You looked wonderful tonight,' Payne said. 'You were really professional. You could carry on modelling if you wanted.'

Charmaine laughed. 'Oh no. Once was enough. Never again.'

Besides, there'd be no reason to go on with this farce once she was back in England.

The thought of going back to Oxfordshire held no appeal anymore, and the thought saddened her. Once, her little cottage and pretty garden, Wordsworth and her work had been her entire universe and more than enough to keep her happy.

Now though, with the exception of Wordsworth, she felt she could give up all the rest tomorrow without a moment's regret. If only this man would say he loved her.

'Why don't you stay?' Payne said, startling her nearly out of her wits because, just for a moment, she was convinced that it was her own mind that had asked the question out loud.

'Oh no. No, I couldn't do that,' she said at last.

'Why not? You can design clothes here as well as anywhere. Who knows — the Bahamas might even inspire you to greater heights,' he pointed out.

'I have a cat,' she said flatly, then jumped as he burst out laughing.

'Well you can always bring your cat over here. What's her name?'

'His name is Wordsworth. He's a black and white long-haired.'

'I'd like to meet him,' Payne said seriously, although his eyes, when she looked up at him, were twinkling.

Charmaine knew that the likelihood of Payne ever meeting her beloved pet were virtually nil. Now the shoot was over, the girls would be flying back after a few days' holiday, and she would go with them.

And never see this man again.

'It's late,' she said abruptly, her voice unknowingly harsh and brittle.

'Is that a polite way of asking me to go?' Payne mused dryly.

'Perhaps. But I thought you'd be only too pleased to go. You've been doing your best to make it clear you want to keep some distance between us,' she snapped, then stopped, appalled.

How had she let her own pain make her blurt out her sense of injury like that? What was wrong with her? But to her incredulity, he didn't try to deny it. Instead he looked at her long and levelly for a few moments, then nodded.

'Yes, I suppose I have,' he said at last, with devastating honesty. 'The thing is, I feel so guilty still, and I'm not used to it. I felt like such a heel over that shark business that I told myself I'd never let anything like it happen again. It seemed the only way was to keep you at arm's length. But it doesn't seem to be working, does it?' he added ruefully, and looked down at her, so close beside him that he could feel her hair brush against his skin as the sea breeze fanned the long silvery locks against his forearms.

All he had to do was reach out and there she'd be — warm and sensuous, a honey trap no man would ever regret falling into.

Charmaine gaped at him. 'Guilty? But why? I mean, you have nothing to feel guilty about. Anyway—'

She came to an abrupt stop.

'Anyway what?' he all but whispered, but she was already drawing away from him and shaking her head.

'Oh nothing. It doesn't matter.'

For a second he was silent, as if giving her a chance to change her mind or tell him something. Then he seemed to sigh heavily.

'So we're calling a truce then?' he asked gently.

'Yes, a truce,' Charmaine heard herself repeating, even if against her better judgement.

'In that case, how about a picnic tomorrow? I know just the place. I'll pick you up at eleven?'

Charmaine nodded weakly. She knew she should have put him off and made an excuse. She knew she was only prolonging the inevitable and letting herself in for more heartache this way, but she just couldn't resist it.

A few more hours in his company. A little while longer to hear his voice and bask in his attention. Surely it wasn't too much to ask?

Lucy need never know.

'All right, eleven,' she said softly.

CHAPTER TEN

Payne headed west from the hotel, knowing the perfect scenic spot for their picnic. Every now and then he glanced across at Charmaine, wondering what she was thinking, and believing that now, at last, he had a pretty good idea.

The thing was, what should he do about it?

'You're quiet today,' he observed, changing the sports car down into a lower gear as they toiled up a steep incline. 'Nothing wrong is there?'

'No,' Charmaine said instantly. 'What could be wrong?'

'Oh, I don't know,' Payne shrugged, and when she still didn't speak, sighed quietly to himself. Well, he'd given her every chance to come clean. But since she seemed determined to keep on her chosen path, he had no choice but to follow her along it. But that didn't mean to say he wasn't going to influence the direction it took. Or throw up a few interesting diversions along the way!

As he parked up, the spectacular view of the wild, wind-swept coastline almost took Charmaine's breath away. The spot he chose was a hollow in an open field, in the shelter of a large tree which kept them discreetly hidden from any other visitors roaming about on this part of the island.

Charmaine watched him take a large picnic hamper from the back of the car and then followed somewhat nervously. All around gulls and other inshore birds sang and called, while under her feet, wild flowers grew in profusion. She couldn't see the ocean, but could both hear and smell it, its evocative presence a constant seduction.

Payne had tossed a fleecy red and black plaid blanket over his arm and now he flung it out, covering the grass and flowers, before slipping onto his knees and reaching into the basket.

'I hope you like Buck's Fizz,' he said, bringing out a cooler. 'I had the chef squeeze the oranges fresh from the tree this morning, and the Brut is from a friend of mine in France who always ships over a crate of his best every year.'

Charmaine sank down on the other side of the blanket and nodded. 'It sounds wonderful,' she said, and reached for a blade of grass and plucked it restlessly.

She was wearing a pale lemon summer dress in faux silk with a silver and blue geometric pattern. With her long fair hair falling loose, and her blue eyes bluer than the sky, she looked more beautiful than Payne could ever remember seeing her appear before — even when in full 'model' make-up and cutting-edge designer chic.

'Let's see — we have cracked crab and salad, little lobster patties, cold whole roasted quail and prosciutto and figs.'

Charmaine watched him take out cutlery and real bone china plates, and a couple of fluted crystal glasses, and couldn't help but smile. Back home, a picnic meant a few sandwiches and a piece of cake! She sighed with pleasure as she bit into a ripe, juicy fig, and Payne watched her appreciatively as he dished up for them both.

'There's what looks like fruit soaked in kirsch for dessert,' he said, delving back into the hamper, 'and I think . . .' he pulled off the lid of a sealed dish, 'yes, apricot snow.'

Charmaine had no idea what that was, and when he glanced up and caught her wry smile, challenged softly, 'What?'

She shrugged. 'Nothing. It's just that . . . well, you live in a different world.' She waved a hand helplessly over the magnificent spread. Just how did she explain that all of this was like a dream?

Payne nodded, and pushing his plate to one side, sat forward and contemplatively leaned his forearms on his raised knees. He was wearing a pair of immaculately tailored beige slacks and a white and beige shirt. He looked too good to be true.

But right now, he was frowning slightly. 'I know just what you mean,' he said at last. 'But it's not really real, you know.'

Charmaine frowned in puzzlement. 'What do you mean? Not real?'

Payne grinned across at her, his grey eyes thoughtful. 'Did I ever tell you that I was born in what had once been a small mining town in Wales? No? Well, I was, and at least half the population were on the dole after the pits closed.' He too reached down and plucked a blade of grass.

He'd never unburdened his soul to a woman before, but, surprisingly, he felt very little fear or unease. And yet, perhaps he wasn't so surprised at that. Charmaine was like none of his previous women. And for certain, the same rules no longer applied!

'I went to the local comprehensive school, which was understaffed, and pretty grim,' he confessed, without drama or self-pity. 'I left at sixteen, packed my bags and never looked back.' He sighed. 'I was young and had nothing to lose. Why not? I started backpacking around Europe, taking the odd job here and there, learning more about life than any A-level syllabus could teach me.'

Charmaine nodded, fascinated. Her own childhood had been a bed of roses by comparison. She'd always lived in the beauty of the English countryside, cushioned by her family, and had always been well taken care of.

'It was interesting, and taught me a lot,' Payne said, and something in his voice made Charmaine suspect that he was leaving out a lot of the harder realities.

'And one of the things I learned was that I was lucky,' he went on smoothly. 'I mean, really lucky. It began by playing cards one night in this Italian youth hostel. I'd never really played cards before — not for money. Not seriously. But I won that night. Not a lot, just a can of Coke and the best bed in the dorm.' He shrugged and smiled in remembrance, then tossed the blade of grass away. 'After that I played again and again, and won far more often than I lost. I began to see it as a talent. Just like some people have a flair for cookery, or can sketch a perfect tree, I saw my luck at gambling in the same way. So, if people who can cook can train hard and become chefs, and people who can draw become artists or take courses to go into related fields like advertising or architecture, why shouldn't I use my edge in exactly the same way? So I left Italy and headed for Monaco, my equivalent of Oxford or Yale.'

Charmaine stared at him curiously. 'And what happened there?'

'I got a job in the casino,' Payne said. 'I watched, and listened and learned. But never placed a single bet. Not the whole time I was there.'

Charmaine frowned. 'Why not?'

'Because I'd realised by then that I wanted to be more than an itinerant gambler. I wanted to gamble for fun, for pleasure, just to see how far I could push it. And I still do that, every now and then.'

'Hence the car,' Charmaine said, in sudden understanding. 'What did you use to bet against it?' she just had to ask.

Payne grinned. 'The *Queen of Diamonds*,' he said quietly.

Charmaine gasped. 'But she's worth far more than the car.'

'I know. That's why her owner snapped up the bet. But as you see, I ended up with both car and yacht. But that's what I was talking about just now — that was just for the sheer hell of it,' Payne explained, knowing that it was important that she understand. 'But I realised very early on that you can't build a life on that. That's why I went into business. Hotels, luxury cars, commodities for a while, and eventually came into the casino itself — ironically because of a gamble.'

He laughed, then sighed. 'But do you know what I did, the first time I had some serious money in my pocket? I bought my mum and dad, and my sister and her husband, a semi-detached house each in Aberystwyth. That was real. Owning the Palace wasn't. Do you see the difference?'

Charmaine nodded simply. 'Yes.'

'So this picnic — it's fancy, it's luxurious, it's a fantasy meal, but it's not real in the same way as eating a really good Cornish pasty when you're starving hungry. So I live in the Bahamas and love it, and run the casino and it makes me happy, but I never make the mistake of thinking that my life depends on it.'

'No,' she said softly. What a remarkable man this was. All this time she'd been thinking of him as a shallow playboy with no real values or understanding of humanity, when in reality he'd grasped truths that, until now, she'd never even thought of. Or had to think of.

'The thing is,' Payne said, 'life is risky. So when you find something worthwhile you grab it with both hands and never let go.' He looked at her keenly. Did she understand what he was saying? Had she realised that she was being given fair warning?

Charmaine sighed. That's all right if you have the courage, she thought sadly. Or had only yourself to consider. But not everyone could afford such a bold policy.

'That's why I bought this,' he went on, making her look up in surprise. He was already pulling a small square box from his slacks pocket, and when he opened the lid with a casual flick of his thumb, exposing a beautiful square-cut Ceylon sapphire surrounded by diamonds, she felt stunned.

She stared at the ring in utter stupefaction.

'Will you marry me, Charmaine?' Payne asked softly.

* * *

Years could have passed. Or seconds. She couldn't tell. Slowly, things became familiar again. The touch of the hot

113

Caribbean sun on her skin, the song of the birds, the sensation of her own breathing.

'Wh-wh-what did you say?' she managed to blurt out at last. Perhaps she'd been dreaming, or had fallen asleep for an instant, or gone suddenly insane.

'I want you to marry me,' Payne repeated, his voice, for a man proposing marriage, sounding curiously calm and almost emotionless.

Charmaine dragged her eyes from the most beautiful ring she'd ever seen and forced herself to meet his eyes. Instantly she was drowning in their soft grey depths.

'But, but, why?' she finally demanded. It was the only thing she could think of to ask. Things were out of control, and she had no idea what was happening. Things like this just didn't happen to her.

'Because we fit together,' Payne said simply. 'I knew it the moment I first saw you, in the garden. When you mistook me for a mere humble gardener.'

Charmaine flushed.

'I knew then you were special, but I didn't want to admit it to myself. Afterwards, I tried to think of you as just another one of the models, someone who'd be here today and gone tomorrow. But I just couldn't make you insignificant. You had a way of becoming the most important thing in my life, and you just wouldn't quit.'

Charmaine swallowed a painful, dry lump in her throat. So she'd succeeded. She'd come here determined to make Payne fall for her, and here he was, telling her that she'd done just that.

And yet her victory was nothing but dust.

'I can tell by the way you're falling over yourself to say yes that my argument is winning you over,' Payne said dryly. 'So I'll tell you what. I'll keep this for now — but I want you to promise to think it over. We may have only known each other a short time, but I'm deadly serious about this.'

He hoped, after what he'd just told her, that she'd be convinced to make the right choice. He was going to have her, no matter what. It was as simple, as basic, as that.

She almost cried out in pain as he snapped the lid shut on the ring and thrust the little box back into his pocket. She had to curl her fingers into fists to stop herself from reaching out and snatching it back. Her engagement ring finger was almost throbbing, as if sensing the ghostly presence of the enclosing circle.

'I have to warn you though,' Payne said, suddenly moving across the blanket until he was only inches away from her, 'that I won't take no for an answer.'

And then he kissed her.

Charmaine felt his weight remorselessly and wonderfully pressing her down onto the blanket, his sweeping arm scattering the containers of food away onto the grass.

She moaned beneath his lips, shuddering as his hand moved up the length of her bare thigh, over her waist and came around to cup one breast. Through the thin material of her dress, her nipple burgeoned with silent begging. He lifted his lips from hers, allowing her to drag in a much-needed breath, but it was only so he could trail tiny kisses along the length of her jaw and nibble her ear lobe, before raining kisses down the side of her neck and crossing her throat to give her the same treatment on the other side.

Above her the azure sky spun in giddy swirls, and she gasped as his other hand slipped beneath the hem of her dress and caressed her inner thigh tormentingly. As if answering to the code of some magic marauder, her thighs parted and she cried out as his fingers pressed against the material of her panties, finding the outline of her femininity and rubbing against her a knowing, tantalising message with his fingers.

She shuddered and gasped out his name, the tension inside her flooding out in a warm ooze that left her feeling boneless.

When he at last lifted his head to look down at her, his eyes were blazing, and a hot flush coloured his high cheekbones. He looked incredibly sexy.

Wordlessly, she lifted one hand to cup it behind his head and pull him down to her breast, where he licked and kissed her nipples through the silk. She whimpered, badly wanting the touch of him on her bare flesh, but suddenly he sat up, running a shaking hand through his tousled blond hair, and grinning down at her.

'When we're married,' he said ominously, his voice thick and slightly slurred, 'you won't get off so lightly.'

She stared at him numbly as he packed up the remains of the picnic, and then, when he stood above her holding out his hand, she let him pull her unresistingly to her feet.

She felt utterly bemused. Her body was still clamouring wantonly for more, but already she was beginning to feel ashamed. Ashamed and just a little scared.

She had a tiger by the tail, and was damned if she knew what to do with him!

'Come on, we'd best get back,' he said almost grimly. He stashed the hamper then opened the door for her, watching her intently as she stumbled into her seat.

She looked shell-shocked, and he knew just how she felt. He was feeling a bit blasted himself. But at least now he had the answer to two very important questions.

Firstly, that she wanted him, every bit as much as he wanted her. And secondly, she was not so hell-bent on revenge that she'd snapped up his offer of marriage just like that. Which meant, which had to mean, that she must have some sort of kinder feelings for him after all.

Now all he had to do was find the best way to make use of both of these fascinating and heart-thumping pieces of information. Which was not something that a man of his talents should find too challenging. In fact, it wasn't until they were nearly back at Paradise Beach that the answer suddenly came to him.

They were parked at a T-junction when he looked across at a billboard announcing Saturday's celebration of his ownership of the Palace. It promised all who came a spectacular night of once-in-a-lifetime gambling opportunities, entertainment, food and wine, and suddenly he knew. It was perfect. Like a gift from Lady Luck herself.

When Charmaine looked across at him, she felt her world lurch on its axis. Why was he smiling like that? He looked like an art collector who'd just stumbled on a hitherto unknown Da Vinci. What did it mean?

And how was she to get herself out of this mess?

* * *

When she reached the top of the stairs, she was glad of the hotel's air conditioning. As it was, she felt almost too tired to trudge the few yards to her door.

She was glad that Payne had simply dropped her off at the entrance with a brief, breathtaking kiss, for she simply didn't know how to cope with him now. If he'd walked her to the door she just knew that they'd have spent the afternoon in bed, and now that she'd had a taste of what bliss that would be, she was sufficiently self-aware to admit that there was no way she'd ever be able to deny him.

With a sigh that was half relieved, half disappointed, she opened the door, walked in, then stopped dead.

'Lucy!' she breathed.

And there, indeed, was her sister, sitting on the edge of her bed, restlessly flipping over the pages of a magazine.

'Sis!' Lucy grinned, tossing aside the magazine and walking over to hug her. 'You look like a stunned mullet! I hope you don't mind — I sort of bribed one of the maids to let me in.' She smiled at her sister in puzzlement. 'You are glad to see me, aren't you?'

Charmaine, aware that she was being less than welcoming, abruptly snapped out of it. 'Of course I am. Of course! It's just that I never expected to see you here.'

If her sister but knew it, she was just one shock too many. Charmaine felt punch drunk.

'Glad to hear it, sis, because I'm booked in right next door,' Lucy chirruped.

For a heart-stopping moment, Charmaine thought she meant that she was staying in the Palace. Then her sister waved a hand at the far wall. 'In the next room in fact, so if

117

I hold a wild party, don't go banging on the wall and yelling for me to shut up! Well, actually, you'd be at the party as well, so you wouldn't be yelling for quiet, you'd be in there helping us make all the noise, so . . .' Lucy paused for a much-needed breath, and Charmaine felt herself giggling.

It was always this way with her sister. She had such a zest for life that she was always dragging her shy sibling into scrapes and situations way beyond her. But why had she come back? Try as she might, Charmaine just couldn't understand why her sister would want to come back to the same island as the man who'd almost destroyed her.

'So, how's the shoot been going?' Lucy demanded, bouncing back down onto the bed, but eyeing her sister closely. 'I saw Jo-Jo on the way in, at reception. He was telling me that you're actually doing some of the modelling.'

'Don't sound so surprised,' Charmaine laughed, trying to look nonchalant. 'I'm not that bad at it. Well, I was a bit inexperienced at first, but I think Phil was pleased with me, which is all that matters.'

Lucy crossed her legs and swung one foot in a tell-tale gesture. Charmaine knew that particular piece of body language from old, and felt her spirits sink. Lucy scented a mystery, and she was not the kind of woman to let a mystery pass her by. Even as a little girl, she'd always sought out her Christmas presents, no matter how carefully their parents tried to hide them, and opened them to see what was inside.

'Jo-Jo was surprised I didn't know,' Lucy mused, looking up from an apparently disinterested inspection of her fingernails — painted in a rainbow of colours — and snared her sister with a sharp glance.

'He always thought you told me everything. And until now, so did I.'

Charmaine couldn't mistake the hurt tone underneath the banter, and she bit her lip.

'I just didn't want you to know in case I made a fool of myself,' she lied frantically. 'You know how it is. Ideas that seem good at the time slowly begin to look like a mistake.

118

Well, this was one of those. I thought it would help me break out of my rut. It seemed like such fun — model a few of my own clothes, take an exotic holiday at the same time, kick over the traces. But then I began to worry I wouldn't be any good, so I decided not to mention it to you or Dad.'

Lucy shook her head wryly. 'You are a dope. I keep on telling you and telling you that you're a born star, and still you persist in doing yourself down. Of course you were a hit. I bet that spiteful redhead you use is howling at the moon.'

Charmaine chortled. 'She is a bit,' she said, with understandable glee.

Lucy laughed. Then her eyes narrowed. 'So, what made you choose the Bahamas?'

Charmaine swallowed hard. This could get tricky. Lucy was no fool. 'Oh, well, you had something to do with it actually. You told me how great this place was when you came back off holiday a few months ago. Remember?'

Lucy watched as her sister walked to the dressing table and kicked off her shoes, refusing to meet her eyes. She always knew when Charmaine was lying. She was always so hopeless at it. Unlike herself, who could and did lie regularly, and very well indeed.

'So, what brings *you* back?' Charmaine asked, unable to bear it any longer. She simply had to know. 'Another holiday is it? It's not like you to go to the same place twice. I thought you said the next vacation you took was going to be to Bangkok or Singapore?'

She glanced up at her sister's reflection in the mirror just in time to see the look on Lucy's face, and her heart jolted.

Her sister looked grim, and yet resolute. Like someone about to face something unpleasant. And yet, at the same time, she looked excited. Almost radiant. She turned slowly, a sense of fear and dread beginning to rise up in her throat.

'Oh, I'm not here on holiday,' Lucy said at last.

'No?' Charmaine croaked.

Lucy shook her head, then looked up, smiling.

'Charmaine, I'm here to get back the man I love.'

CHAPTER ELEVEN

Charmaine groped behind her for the chair and sank down abruptly. 'Y-you've come back for . . .' She almost said Payne's name out loud but stopped herself just in time, remembering that, as far as Lucy was aware, her sister knew nothing about her doomed love affair.

'The man I love, yes,' Lucy said, with a defiant lift of her chin. 'I know I never told you this, sis, but when I came here before, I met someone,' Lucy said, still with a kind of stiff-necked pride that made Charmaine wonder why she was being so defensive.

Unless, of course, she was ashamed to be admitting that she was actually chasing after a man. Usually men chased Lucy. So Charmaine could imagine that she might be feeling a little humiliated to be confessing to her sister that a man had dumped her, and that she was now the one doing the pursuing.

'I see,' she said hollowly. 'And are you . . . are you absolutely sure that he loves you?' she asked, trying to find a way to let Lucy down lightly. Because of one thing she was sure — Payne Lacey had not missed her. Not one little bit. And she was in a unique position to know!

'Oh yes, I'm sure of that,' Lucy said, then laughed a little uneasily. 'The thing is, sis, things got a bit . . . messy, I suppose you could say. There were circumstances that made everything so horrible.'

Charmaine bit her lip and glanced away. Horrible wasn't the word for it.

When Lucy had come back from her holiday to the Bahamas, Charmaine had known at once that something was wrong — dreadfully wrong. Lucy, usually so effervescent and so sure of herself, seemed lacklustre and distracted. Worse, she'd then failed an audition that both Charmaine and their father knew she should have aced, and had proceeded to mope about her flat without any make-up on, barely eating and generally going into a decline. She had insisted she didn't want to talk about it.

Then Charmaine had begun to hear rumours. Although Lucy had a wide range of friends and Charmaine didn't run around in their circle, she knew people who did, and soon it was reaching her ears that Lucy had had a wild affair in the Bahamas with a casino-owning playboy who'd dumped her. Hard. To make matters even harder, there had been a certain maliciousness in these rumours, for Lucy, popular with both men and women alike, had always had easy conquests before, and there was a certain amount of self-satisfaction that she'd at last got her comeuppance.

Naturally, Charmaine hadn't let on to her sister that she knew about Payne Lacey. Nor did she tell Lucy how everyone was pseudo-sympathising with her behind her back. If Lucy didn't want to talk, there was no point forcing her. But when the need had arisen for an exotic swimwear shoot for Jonniee, so too had Charmaine's plan. She had been determined to put the smile back on her little sister's face.

So why did she feel as if she was dying inside?

Well, duh! It didn't take a genius to figure that out, did it, she told herself grimly, as Lucy began to chatter about all the good times they'd have in the next three days, which was all Charmaine had left on the island.

If Lucy was determined to have something, Lucy always got it. Maybe even Payne Lacey. She was a tenacious human dynamo when she was this emphatic, and what man could resist Lucy in full battle-cry? After all, she had all of an actress's weapons right at her disposal, not to mention her moral right of a prior claim on him.

It was not as if Charmaine could, or should, compete with her.

At this, Charmaine brought herself up short. Compete with Lucy? Now where had that thought come from? Of course she wouldn't compete with her sister. Apart from anything else, Lucy had seen him first.

Something about this struck her as childish, and she had to fight an inane desire to giggle.

As Lucy began to talk about taking a boat out to one of the smaller islands, Charmaine tried to force herself to listen. But all she could think about was Payne. How would he react to Lucy's return? After all, their affair couldn't have been totally one-sided. He must have had feelings for her. And Lucy wasn't someone easily forgotten. And even if he had thought the affair was over, and wasn't best pleased to see an ex-lover appear over the horizon — especially since he seemed to be in hot pursuit of another conquest, namely herself! — how long would it be before Lucy was reminding him of all he had missed?

She knew her sister was a sophisticated and scintillating woman, and must be a fabulous lover. She knew a lot of famous people, and had theatrical stories to tell and a store of gossip that delighted even the most jaded listener. What's more she could become beautiful, mysterious or tragic at the drop of a hat.

How long before she herself began to fade into insignificance, and Payne regretted his proposal of marriage to her?

She would never wear that lovely ring.

At this wayward thought, she leapt up and began to pace the room. She was so distracted she didn't notice that her sister had broken off her sightseeing plans and was watching her with growing concern.

Charmaine went to the French windows and looked out restlessly. How stupid could she be? Of course she was never going to wear the ring. She couldn't do that to Lucy, especially not now she'd arrived to claim Payne back for herself.

Charmaine had to face it: she was never going to marry Payne Lacey.

'Hey, Planet Earth calling Charmaine Reece. Is anyone out there?'

Charmaine blinked then spun around, forcing herself to laugh lightly. 'Sorry, did I zone out for a while?'

'I'll say. All the way to Jupiter by the look of it. Is something wrong?' Lucy asked.

'No of course not,' Charmaine said, with her best newly learned model's smile. What could possibly be wrong?

'You look like hell,' Lucy said, coming towards her and looping a consoling arm around her shoulders. It was almost more than Charmaine could bear. 'What is it with this island? It seems to be cursed for both of us. What's wrong? Is it a man at last?'

Charmaine swallowed hard, avoiding her sister's kind, sympathetic eyes. 'No. You know me. No man trouble.'

Lucy nodded, but she didn't look convinced. 'Well, as soon as I've got my little problem sorted out, we'll work on yours, OK? Remember, nobody messes with the two musketeers and wins,' she said, shaking a fist in the air as they used to as children.

At this remembrance of childhood solidarity, Charmaine only managed not to burst into tears by offering to help her sister unpack, and grimly thrusting every thought from her head. It left her feeling curiously numb, but numb, after a day like this, was just what she needed.

* * *

It was the biggest gala night the Palace had ever seen. And it had seen some grand nights in its time. The best caterers on the island had been hired to provide food, and the legendary cellar belonging to the previous casino owner had been liberally poached to provide the finest in vintages. A New Orleans jazz band provided evocative memories of the Roaring Twenties.

Some tables had been granted a special licence for higher gambling stakes, so that a large crowd had gathered around a Thai businessman and an American computer pioneer who were regularly making bets of half a million dollars.

There was a heady, anything-can-happen atmosphere, coupled with an elegant recklessness that reminded Charmaine of a 1930s lavish Hollywood production. She half expected Greta Garbo to waltz through the gambling rooms trailing smoke from an ivory cigarette holder, a bevy of men in her wake.

Anyone who was anyone was here. And a lot of people had flown in from all over the globe for the once-in-a-blue-moon gambling opportunity. More than one person could be overheard wondering how Payne had managed to get the gaming commission to let him slip the leash for the night.

'Isn't he scared someone will break the bank?' was one of the first things Charmaine and Lucy overheard as they walked through the front door and passed through the marble foyer.

'Not him,' someone else said. 'The man's got nerves of steel.'

Charmaine stole a quick glance at her sister, wondering what she was thinking. But Lucy looked merely excited and intrigued, and not at all worried that her former lover seemed to be taking one of his legendary enormous gambles.

'This is just like Payne,' Lucy said matter-of-factly as they made their way through the crowds to watch a game of roulette. 'Max always said he was half mad.'

So Lucy knew Max. Well, that was hardly surprising. Charmaine had learned over the last few days that Max Galway was one of Payne's oldest friends on the island. Naturally, he and Lucy would have met.

'Look, there's Jo-Jo and the gang,' Lucy added, nodding across the acreage of room to where the models were clustered around a crap shoot. From the screaming encouragement and the wild groans that were echoing from over there, the dice players must be playing for heart-stopping odds.

It was almost midnight, but they were hardly late. This had all the makings of an all-night session which would, in time, turn into the stuff of legend or fable.

'Someone's just won two million in the baccarat room,' some woman screamed in excitement to her companion, but such was the scale of the night that this was barely news. Later, Charmaine heard someone else say that a Korean gentlemen had lost ten million.

It was so crowded that it took nearly an hour for Charmaine to even spot Payne. He was dressed in black, not a tuxedo, but a plain jacket with silver buttons and elegant slacks. With his fair hair and steely grey eyes he stood out amongst the gaudily garbed crowd.

She herself was wearing a smoky lavender gown, one of her own creations, in gauzy chiffon. With it, she wore a single pear-drop amethyst necklace on chain so fine it was almost invisible and a pair of silver-grey heels. She had her hair up in what she called a 'Lucy special'. It was one of the intricate hair designs that Lucy had learned while doing a period drama for the BBC, and she had woven real and freshly flown-over violets that looked wonderful in Charmaine's silvery hair. Even Lucy had been speechless when the two girls had finished making themselves up.

Her sister was in a figure-hugging short scarlet cocktail dress, with brightly painted nails and bold lipstick. Of the two, Charmaine was convinced that everyone looked at Lucy first, then at herself as a poor second.

But when she felt eyes resting on her, and turned to find Payne just yards away, staring at her over the cowed heads of several poker players, she knew he was looking at her. Avidly.

And not at her sister.

Instantly, she tensed. This was the moment she was dreading. The first time Lucy and Payne met again.

At least, as far as Charmaine knew. Lucy would've told her if she'd already seen him, wouldn't she? Or would she? What if they'd already spent the night together?

She felt jealousy, as cruel as the grave, eat at her soul and forced herself to swallow it back.

She watched, helpless with longing and taut with fear, as he wove his way towards them.

When he was almost there, Lucy turned around and the smile on her face wobbled and fell. She looked suddenly as tense as Charmaine felt.

'Hello, Payne,' Lucy said the moment he was in earshot, almost as if anxious to get in the first word. She looked nervous and unsure of herself, things that Charmaine would previously have thought impossible of her sister.

'Hello, Lucy,' Payne said neutrally.

Charmaine, who'd been straining to hear even the slightest intonation of his voice, would have sworn he sounded reserved. Like someone meeting an acquaintance he didn't know very well. Moreover, an acquaintance he wasn't sure he wanted to cultivate.

It stunned her. What was going on? Surely he wasn't cold-shouldering her? After all that she'd learned about him, she would never have put him down as a boor.

'Thanks for letting me come,' Lucy further stunned her by saying politely. 'I know I'm probably the last person you wanted to see here, but Charmaine wouldn't come without me.'

Well, that was true enough. When she'd told Lucy that she and all the Jonniee gang had standing invitations to this bash-of-the-century, Lucy had demurred, pointing out that she had no invitation herself and doubtless wouldn't be let through the door. So Charmaine had asked Jo-Jo if he could wangle another invite, unwilling to talk to Payne herself. And sure enough, within the hour, an extra invitation had appeared at the front desk.

But why was Lucy acting so . . . diffidently? It wasn't like her. Even as a child, whenever she'd done something wrong, or incurred the displeasure of an adult, she'd become cheeky and winsome, charming everyone with her aplomb.

But now she was acting . . . well, chastised.

What on earth had gone on between them to make Lucy, Lucy of all people, act like this?

'Don't be silly,' Payne said urbanely. 'You're always welcome at the Palace. Let me get you a drink — champagne cocktail, right?'

And again Charmaine felt her mouth drop open in surprise and had to snap it shut before anyone noticed.

Of course Payne knew Lucy's favourite drink, but why was he making it sound as if he barely knew her?

And then it hit her. It must be for her benefit!

When Jo-Jo had asked him for an extra invite for Charmaine's sister, he'd probably thought nothing of it. But during the night he must have spotted Lucy, seen they were together and quickly added up two and two. Which put him in a mighty fix. How embarrassing to find that the woman you'd just proposed to was the sister of a former lover!

Charmaine looked at Lucy as she accepted the cocktail from Payne. Her sister still had that slightly wary, stiffly embarrassed look on her face.

Her heart ached for Lucy, and when Payne, with a long look at Charmaine, excused himself to go and see whether or not a French count, who was having a remarkable run of luck, was still riding high, she heaved a sigh of relief.

'Lucy, we need to talk,' she said urgently. She was determined to come clean before somebody else let slip about them. But Lucy wasn't listening. Instead she seemed to be staring across the room at somebody.

'What? Oh, yes, later, sis, OK? There's someone I must see.'

'Lucy, are you all right?' Charmaine asked, reaching out to grab her arm and prevent her from taking off.

Startled, Lucy turned to look at her with eyes that Charmaine would have sworn looked genuinely bewildered.

'What do you mean, am I all right? Of course. You're the one who's being weird,' Lucy observed.

'Look, about Payne,' Charmaine began.

'Oh, Payne,' Lucy said, and smiled stiffly. 'Yes, that is a bit embarrassing, isn't it,' she agreed, making Charmaine gape all over again. 'But he's a sport, isn't he?' Lucy swept on, once again looking over her shoulder to the other side of the room. 'And if he's not going to hold a grudge, then that's more than I could have hoped for. Look, sis, I've just got to see this man. I'll find you later, OK?'

And with that, Lucy pulled away and was quickly lost in the crowd.

But Charmaine wasn't fooled. There wasn't someone she was anxious to see — no man she needed to talk to. She just wanted to find a ladies' room where she could cry her eyes out and collect herself.

Charmaine bit her lip and turned blindly away. So much for protecting her sister. So much for not stabbing her in the back. All that soul searching and self-denial was for nothing.

For the past day and night she'd been carefully holding herself back from thinking about Payne's proposal. About what it might, about what it surely must, mean. After all, no man asked a woman to marry him lightly. But neither had Payne actually said he loved her. Not in so many words. Not in a way that left her in no doubt.

But still he'd proposed. And having seen him with Lucy tonight, it was clear his head would not be turned back in her sister's direction.

Payne wanted to marry her! Her, Charmaine Reece. Not Lucy, not Jinx, not any of the other fascinating, beautiful, intelligent women of his past.

And oh how she wanted to accept. If she was brutally honest with herself — and now was probably a good time to be brutally honest — she wanted to marry Payne Lacey more than anything else in the world.

She loved him.

Oh, his lifestyle bemused her, and his cavalier attitude to luck and money still unnerved her. But after their talk at the picnic, even this failed to seriously worry her. Besides, if Payne lost all his money tomorrow on some reckless gamble, she could still support them both. Because of Jonniee she was a wealthy woman in her own right, and would always have the means of supporting herself.

No, only the thought of Lucy's pain had stopped her from seriously thinking about his proposal of marriage. If she accepted, would her sister ever get over it?

Part of her was sure that she would. Nothing kept Lucy down forever. But Charmaine had never seen her so miserable as she was after their break-up. Obviously Payne meant more to her than any of her other conquests.

Oh it was all so impossible, she thought, wanting to scream and cry. For the last couple of weeks she'd felt as if she had been living her life on a rollercoaster — up and down, he loves me, he loves me not, I love him, no I don't. Yes I can, no I can't. It was enough to drive her to the brink of insanity.

And now . . . just what should she do now? Go to her sister? Or go to the man she loved and wanted and who had proposed to her?

She didn't know. She couldn't seem to think. She felt paralysed with uncertainty and torn in half.

And then suddenly, she heard Payne's voice. 'Ladies and gentlemen.'

He was obviously speaking over a microphone, and she half expected him to be stood on a dais somewhere, so she almost jumped when he appeared at her side. 'I hope you're all enjoying the evening's entertainment.'

The crowds began to quieten, some coming in from the other gaming tables to listen to his speech, others too engrossed to care.

Without quite realising it, Payne put a hand on her back and began leading her to one of the roulette tables, still talking into the microphone in his other hand.

'As you're aware, there's been some high-stakes gambling going on tonight, but so far, I think, the bank is safe.'

There were cheers and laughter at this, and a growing sense of anticipation. Clearly Payne Lacey was not the man to make announcements without reason. Something big was in the offing.

'I want to thank you all for making this celebration of my ownership a night to remember. And, in honour of this occasion, I'd like to make a bet myself.'

Suddenly the air became filled with tension as people began to realise that something quite extraordinary was happening. It was common knowledge that Payne never gambled in his own casino. Charmaine felt her own heart begin to pound as she was swept along on the current of anticipation. Looking around she caught glimpses of faces in the crowd — Jo-Jo looking puzzled, Jinx looking angry. Fizz and Dee-Dee standing together looking intrigued. Everyone was wondering the same thing.

What was going on?

'This bet is going to be the biggest gamble of my life. Who knows, depending on its outcome, maybe even the last,' Payne said, and there were gasps all around. Because when a legendary gambler like Payne Lacey talked like this, everyone listened.

Someone had once said that the only time Payne Lacey bluffed was when he was playing poker. Never when he was playing for real.

'Jack, clear the table and spin the wheel,' Payne said to the roulette croupier, who quickly did as he was told. Those who'd been playing didn't even look chagrined at having their game hijacked like this. They were too caught up in the unfolding drama.

'The bet is a simple one,' Payne continued, never raising his voice or sounding unduly excited, but dominating the room and everyone in it, nevertheless. 'This incredibly beautiful young lady by my side is going to call it. Black or red.'

By now you could hear a pin drop. Even the hardened gamblers in the other rooms had sensed something spectacular going on and had come in to watch. For the first and last time in its history, not even the sound of a fruit machine broke the quiet of the Palace's interior.

'If she wins, the entire house is hers,' Payne said, and there was a moment of stunned awe, followed by a whispering surge of disbelief.

Charmaine blinked. What? What was he saying? The house was probably worth tens of millions tonight! Was he mad? Was he . . . ?

'And if I win,' Payne said, suddenly turning from the amazed crowd and holding her eyes with his own, 'then Miss Charmaine Reece will become Mrs Payne Lacey.'

Charmaine felt the room abruptly recede and sway around them, then come once more sharply back into focus.

'No, Payne,' she heard herself whisper. 'You can't. I can't.' It was madness. Insanity.

But Payne was already reaching for the white ball and with a simple toss of his fingers, threw it expertly into the spinning wheel.

'Red or black?' he said, looking at her calmly. And she felt an undeniable compulsion to go along with this. For the first time ever, she thought she understood his affinity for taking a chance.

And yet, she fought it. You couldn't just decide the rest of your life like this. Could you? And yet — why not? Just a few minutes ago, she was torn by indecision, wracked with conflicting desires. Why not let Lady Luck decide for her?

'Black,' she heard someone say.

And since everybody else was holding their breath, it must have been herself.

Payne didn't even turn to watch the roulette wheel, although everybody else watched it in fascination.

Lucy, who'd pushed her way to the front, stared first at her sister then at Payne then at the wheel in utter stupefaction.

But Charmaine couldn't take her eyes from Payne. Could she really let fate decide for her? Could she really just volunteer her heart and the rest of her life on the whim of chance and expect . . .

'It's red!'

Jack, the croupier, called out the result, and from all around them came the sound of sudden thunderous applause.

Charmaine went hot, then cold. She felt him raise her hand and when she looked down, the beautiful sapphire and diamond ring was on her finger.

'I never renege on a bet,' Payne said, raising her hand to his lips and kissing her knuckles tenderly. But his eyes were like steel when they met hers. 'And I won't let you, either,' he warned her silkily.

CHAPTER TWELVE

When she awoke the next morning, the ring felt heavy and alien on her finger, and yet she simply couldn't make herself take it off. Every time she tried, her heart rebelled. Instead, she rolled over in bed and stared blankly at the wall. She had just one more day and night in the Bahamas then she and the rest of the gang were due to fly back to England.

Would she be with them?

She still didn't know the answer to that, one near sleepless night later. Eventually sheer exhaustion had caused her to doze, but if her subconscious had been tackling the problem without her, it didn't seem in any hurry to let her know what it had concluded!

With a weary sigh, she eventually dragged herself out of bed, showered and pulled on a pearl-grey all-in-one jumpsuit with a huge zipper up the front, one of Jo-Jo's post-modernist creations. She rolled the sleeves back to her elbows in a workmanlike gesture and simply pulled her hair back in a ponytail, securing it with a silver scrunchie. She didn't even bother to add make-up.

On anyone else the stark outfit would have looked drably industrial, but with her skin now a richly glowing honey in colour, and with her feminine curves lending the almost shapeless garment dips and hollows in the all the right places, she looked unknowingly and incredibly sexy.

Having made a swift exit from the casino last night, dashing off before anyone could so much as congratulate her, or in Lucy's case question her, it was time for Charmaine to face the music. She walked next door and tapped on the door, and a moment later her sister's groggy voice called out for her to come in.

Lucy's hotel room was an exact replica of her own, done in slightly differing shades, and as she walked to the French windows to draw back the curtains, Lucy burrowed out from beneath the bedclothes.

'What time is it?' she demanded sleepily.

'No idea. Shall I make you some coffee?' Lucy had never been a morning person, and besides that, she'd probably been hitting the champagne cocktails rather heavily last night, after Payne's bombshell.

And who could blame her?

'Huh? Yeah, sure,' Lucy muttered, sitting up and rubbing her hands briskly over her face in an attempt to wake up.

Charmaine returned with the coffee and sat perched on the edge of the bed. 'Lucy, about last night . . .' she began quietly.

Lucy grimaced and blew on her coffee, and took a tentative sip. 'Well, Payne always did know how to grandstand,' she said, then glanced speculatively across her coffee cup at Charmaine. 'But I must say, I didn't think it was your sort of thing.'

Neither did I, until it was happening, Charmaine thought wryly. Because there was no getting around it — Payne's public proposal and outrageous gamble had made her feel nothing if not alive. And extra special. And terrified out of her mind.

Charmaine knew she should be, at the very least, annoyed with him. He knew her well enough to know that she'd die rather than make a public scene, but surely he didn't expect her to accept their engagement in the cold light of day?

The thing was, she was feeling too happy to be mad. And yet, she knew, it couldn't last.

There came a knock on the door, and Charmaine looked up in surprise.

'Oh, that'll be room service,' Lucy said brightly. 'I ordered the fruit salad for breakfast and the morning papers. Be a love and get it, will you?'

'Thank you,' she took the attractively laid-out tray from the beaming waiter and took it over to the bed, then gave him a tip from Lucy's purse.

'Uh-oh, looks like you made the front page of the paper,' Lucy said excitedly. 'They must have run an extra printing to get it out so soon. Still, Payne's news, wherever he goes.'

Charmaine felt a chill run down her spine at her sister's words. She sounded so carefree and almost admiring. Hard to believe it must be eating her up inside.

Nervously Charmaine went back to the bed and perched on the side. 'What are they saying?' she asked fearfully.

'Oh, you know, the usual,' Lucy said, reading avidly. 'Some are wondering what the female population of the island will do now that the Bahamas' most eligible bachelor has finally been snared. Ugh, some tacky hack is giving odds on how long the marriage will last. Bastards! Don't you take any notice. Any fool can see that Payne's fathoms deep in love with you.'

Charmaine winced as both guilt and hope washed over her at her sister's comment, then watched as Lucy tossed the papers aside and reached for her glass of freshly squeezed mango juice.

'You really are a great actress, aren't you?' Charmaine said softly, making Lucy stop, glass midway to her lips, and blink.

'Well, thank you. I think. Look, sis, I don't want you to think I'm interfering but . . . well, are you sure about all this?'

Charmaine took a long, shaky breath. So here it comes at last.

'About what?'

Lucy put down her juice and leaned back against the headboard. 'About what, she says! Payne, silly. Don't get me wrong,' Lucy carried on, leaning forward and reaching out to touch Charmaine's arm tenderly. 'Nobody could be better pleased than me to see you finally taking charge of things and getting yourself a love life. But . . . well, to be honest, I thought you'd choose someone a little more . . . I don't know. Gentle. More your type. I mean, for a first-time effort, Payne Lacey seems so . . .'

'Out of my league?' Charmaine finally came to her rescue, when Lucy realised she couldn't quite think of the right words.

'Yes, exactly. Look, sis, I know these kinds of people. I move in their world. And I know you, and it scares me a little, to think of you out here all alone among the sharks.'

Charmaine nodded. 'So you're warning me off. Is that it?' She could tell this was her sister's way of diplomatically steering her away from Payne — as far as Lucy was concerned, Charmaine didn't know Payne was the one to have broken her heart, and her pride would probably want to keep it that way.

Lucy blinked again, surprised at the edge of hardness she suddenly detected in her sister's voice. She'd never heard Charmaine sound so tough before.

'What's wrong?' she asked sharply. 'I just don't want to see you get hurt, that's all.'

'Oh. So if I was bringing home as a fiancé some nice librarian from Oxford, or a mild-mannered accountant, you'd be happier?'

Lucy gaped. 'What? What's wrong with you? I don't under—'

'Why don't you just say it?' Charmaine finally cried, tired of all the subterfuge and not liking herself very much in that moment at all. But the truth was, she suddenly found herself wanting to fight like a tiger for Payne, even when her opponent was her own sister!

Just what did that say about her?

'Why don't we just have it out once and for all. It's me he wants, not you. And you can't stand it, can you?' Charmaine cried, hating herself even more, yet unable to stop now.

Lucy felt her jaw drop open. She stared at her hard-eyed, stormy-faced sister and slowly, unbelievably, began to smile.

'Wow! Look at you! At last. I still don't get what it is that you're going on about, but I'm glad to see you fighting mad. I was beginning to think you didn't have it in you. Now, what exactly have I done to get you so good and mad?'

Charmaine gazed back, all the anger suddenly draining from her. She simply couldn't play this game with Lucy. It just wasn't in her.

'You know,' she said flatly.

But Lucy was already shaking her head. 'Nuh-uh, not a clue. You'll have to spell it out, I'm afraid.'

Charmaine sighed. 'All right. Have it your way. You came back to the Bahamas to get your lover back, right? You said so.'

Lucy nodded, her eyes bright and alert and still with that unnervingly encouraging smile on her face. 'Right.'

'But Payne wants me. He's proposed. And I'm not giving him up.'

There, she'd said it. She lifted her chin and stared at her sister steadily. For all their lives, Lucy had been the dominant one. The true showman of the family, Daddy's favourite. But now, this time, Charmaine Reece was at last going to come into her own and fight for the man she loved.

And everyone had better watch out, or else!

'OK. So, what's your problem?' Lucy said, sounding genuinely baffled. 'I'm not asking you to give Payne up. I just thought he might be a bit too much for you, that's all. But now I can tell that I needn't worry about that! Wow, sis, when you come out of your shell you really don't do it in half measures, do you? Looking at you now, I'd say it was Payne who had to watch out!'

Charmaine felt a slow, tightening grip gradually squeeze the breath out of her. From somewhere alarm bells began clamouring. Something was off here. Her sister wouldn't carry the charade this far.

'Lucy,' she said slowly. 'You are in love with Payne, aren't you?' she asked at last, almost too afraid to hear the answer.

But the look on her sister's face said it all. She looked astonished. Amazed even.

'Payne? Payne? No! What on earth made you think that?' Lucy gasped.

'Because everyone was saying it!' Charmaine cried, pushed beyond her endurance. 'All your friends were talking about how you'd fallen hard for this casino owner over in the Bahamas and that he'd dropped you. It was no big secret.'

Lucy suddenly clapped a hand to her mouth and looked at her sister with stricken eyes.

'I know,' she finally pulled her hand away and whispered. 'And that's my fault. All my fault,' she confessed. 'When I was over here before, I let everybody think that it was Payne I was involved with. Oh, I didn't deliberately start the rumour, but when I was aware that it was going around, I did everything I could to encourage it. Payne didn't like it when he found out, but, bless him, he acted like the perfect gentleman and never let on the truth.'

Charmaine took several long, deep breaths. Her heart felt as if it was trying to burst out of her chest and sing like a bird, but after all that had been happening to her recently, her mind was still urging caution. There had been too many misunderstandings. She had to get things absolutely straight this time.

'Lucy, what are you going on about? If you weren't involved with Payne, why did you want everyone to think you were?' she demanded.

'To cover up the truth,' Lucy said, a shade sadly. 'Oh, sis, don't tell me off, I couldn't help it, really. I fell head over heels in love with a married man.'

And as her sister gazed at her, silently begging for understanding and forgiveness, it all suddenly clicked into place.

'Max!' Charmaine breathed. 'You fell in love with Max.'

'Right,' Lucy nodded. 'Right next door at the casino, where I met him. Of course, we were ever so discreet because of his wife, and that's why I just let people think it was Payne I was seeing,' Lucy rushed to explain, having the grace to blush. 'But the more it became obvious that this was the real thing for both Max and me, things became more fraught. Although Max and his wife didn't have any children, they had been married a long time, and Max just couldn't bring himself to break the news to Maria. So, in the end, I gave him an ultimatum and went home. But, oh, Charmaine, I was so miserable without him. I thought I'd never see him again. But then, last week, Max came over to England and told me he was getting a divorce. Apparently, he'd been as miserable as me. Well, after that, I just had to come back with him and help him face the music, didn't I? His wife has a lot of friends on the island, and I couldn't let him go through all this alone. It wouldn't be right. So, no matter what people say, Max and I are going to be together.'

And yet again there was that touch of bravado mixed with unease in her sister's voice; but now Charmaine could understand it only too well. Love did things to you — it turned you into a different person, it seemed. Having been willing to fight tooth and nail for Payne, she could hardly condemn her sister for fighting for Max, could she?

'Oh, Luce! I believed the rumours,' she finally confessed. 'I thought Payne Lacey had seduced and dumped you. So I persuaded Jo-Jo to do the next shoot out here and got myself invited along as a model. I had this big plan to go all out for Payne, make him fall for me, and then dump him, just like I thought he'd done to you.'

Lucy stared at Charmaine, amazed. Was this her quiet little country-mouse sister? No, obviously not.

'Well . . . I don't know what to say,' Lucy eventually blurted. 'Thanks, I suppose, for rushing to avenge me. And . . . well, good on you, girl! If this is what it took to get you to start living your life at last then I can't say I'm sorry,' she finished with a spurt of laughter and a huge grin.

Charmaine couldn't help but laugh too, then abruptly groaned. 'Oh but, Lucy, it all went so wrong,' she wailed. 'I fell for him instead! And then he proposed and I thought I had to say no, because of you. Thinking you loved him still, I mean. And then last night happened, and that wild, silly bet, and now . . . well, now I don't know what I'm going to do!' she finished in despair.

Lucy smiled ruefully. 'What a hopeless pair we are when it comes to romance. Still, there's nothing standing in your way now, right?' she pointed out slyly.

And Charmaine gulped at the thought. 'Right,' she agreed. But her heart was pounding like a frightened rabbit.

* * *

Payne glanced up as the office door opened and Charmaine looked around. When she saw he was alone, she pushed open the door and walked in, and Payne gasped at the sheer effrontery of her outfit. On anyone else that grey jumpsuit with the industrial-sized zipper and rolled-back sleeves would look workmanlike and about as sexy as a potato sack.

On her, it set his pulse racing dizzily.

'Hello. I wondered if I could have a word,' she said, sounding unbelievably nervous. 'About last night.'

'Ah yes. The bet you lost,' he said, which was not exactly the start she'd been hoping for. He smiled like a wolf. 'Come on in.'

Charmaine nervously closed the door behind her and looked around the office. It was light and airy, with views across the gardens, acres of beige carpet and a pale wooden desk and matching filing cabinets. Bright splashes of artwork, scenes of the islands done by a local artist, brightened up the room.

And, taking up one whole wall . . . She stopped dead in her tracks and gaped at it.

It was a giant print of herself, taken that first day on the beach. She was in the swimsuit with the beach robe lapping around her feet in the waves. As a fashion shot it was hopeless, of course — one of her many mistakes.

'Phil presented it to me this morning as a wedding present. He must have been up all night getting it done,' Payne said, his voice husky with emotion.

He too was staring at the picture, at her face, which had a sensual, almost haunted quality. Charmaine remembered what she'd been thinking when Phil had snapped it, and felt her heart contract.

For the first time, she saw herself as Payne and Phil saw her, and realised that she was beautiful.

But what would Payne say now if she'd told him that, at the moment that picture was being taken, she was plotting his downfall?

She dragged her eyes away from the picture with some effort.

'I wondered what Jinx was up to in here the other night,' she said the first thing that came into her mind, then could have bitten off her tongue. Why had she blurted that out? What did it matter now? She sounded like a jealous fish wife!

'Jinx?' Payne said. 'Oh,' he added, and grinned. 'Don't worry, darling. When that red-haired virago was in here — and she's only been in here the once — so was Mrs Simms.'

'Mrs Simms?'

'My secretary. Seventy, feisty, and more than a match for mischief-making redheads, believe me.'

Charmaine nodded. So Jinx was just up to her usual tricks, trying to create the impression of an intimate and satisfying little tête-à-tête. She must have known Charmaine would be watching out for Payne — Jinx was an expert on the all's-fair-in-love-and-war game.

Charmaine dismissed Jinx from her mind once and for all.

'So, about last night?' Payne prompted. 'I hope you're not trying to back out of it, because I won't let you,' he warned, leaning against his desk and watching her like a hawk. 'You had a fifty-fifty chance of escape, just as I had a fifty-fifty chance of losing my shirt.'

Charmaine shook her head. 'Oh, Payne, you're hopeless,' she sighed helplessly. Why didn't he just kiss her? Tell her he loved her. That's all she wanted.

'There's no way in the world you can make me honour that bet,' she said instead.

'Don't be so sure,' he said softly, dangerously. 'You made the wager of your own free will, and in front of witnesses. If I had to, I could drag you into court.'

Charmaine snorted. Perhaps once such a threat would have had her going all a-tremble, but the new, improved Charmaine Reece wasn't about to let it go unchallenged.

'Rot. No judge would ever try and impel a woman to marry against her will and you know it,' she said scornfully.

Slowly, Payne left the desk and came towards her. He moved like a golden mountain lion, all easy grace and effortless power. She backed up a step instinctively, although her suddenly racing heart had little to do with fear and much more to do with desire.

'Maybe not. But I could always sue you for breach of promise,' he husked. But she could tell he was teasing.

Wasn't he? The thing was, she was never sure when he was bluffing and when he wasn't!

Charmaine gasped. 'You wouldn't?'

'No, I wouldn't,' he said, but there was little comfort to be had from that, for he was already reaching out for her. And with a swift movement that had her squealing in surprise, he lifted her into the air and spun her around, taking a few steps and sitting her firmly on the big desk.

He pressed forward, nudging her legs apart and standing so close she could feel his body heat, his fingers curling sensuously around her upper arms.

'Besides, I can think of far more pleasurable ways of persuading you to honour our bet,' he murmured and swooped.

Papers scattered as he lay her across the desk, his fingers going instantly to the tantalising zip and pulling it down.

142

'I've been itching to do that from the moment you walked through the door,' he confessed huskily.

She wore no bra underneath, and she gasped as the warmth of his breath feathered over her naked skin, before gentle, knowing fingers eased the grey material from her shoulders, leaving her gloriously naked to his feasting eyes.

He groaned as he watched her rose-coloured nipples burgeon and tighten as he tweaked them with his fingers.

'You're so beautiful,' he said, lowering his head to slip one throbbing bud deep into his mouth. Her back arched compulsively off the desk, but his superior weight and strength kept her firmly anchored to the wood.

Charmaine gasped. She'd never expected it to feel this good.

'Payne,' she breathed, but with a small moan he moved his lips to her other breast and she shuddered all over again. When she felt him pulling the jumpsuit down, she lifted her hips briefly off the desk in order to let him strip it from her completely, co-operating willingly in her own seduction.

She felt as if she had been waiting for this all her life. Probably because she *had* been waiting for this all her life!

He let the grey material fall to the ground and began to trail hot kisses over her stomach, dipping enticingly into her navel and making her legs thrash in instant response. Then his mouth moved across her brief white panties, his breath hot against the very core of her femininity, and she felt herself began to burn, a hot flush that slowly turned her insides to quivering liquid. His hands were firm on her calves as he pulled her legs ruthlessly apart and she cried out as he began to nibble against her, his tongue, through the lace of her panties, finding the most sensitive part of her and laving ferociously.

Without becoming aware of it she began to undulate on the desk in time with his mouth, and a low groan of sheer wanton desire escaped her lips

A tightening, deepening, ever-hardening core of tension built inside her, demanding release and when it finally came she arched her neck and moaned out his name. Shaking, she watched him move back up her body, his hands pulling the lace panties down as he did so, leaving her totally naked. She'd never been more aware of the vast difference in their sexual experience, but she trusted him totally.

He shrugged off his shirt, and immediately her hands went to his shoulders, exploring the warmth of his skin, the softness of velvet over iron, her hands lovingly tracing the contours of his muscles. She saw his face tighten at the touch and realised, with something like awe, that she could do to him what he had just done to her.

This sense of power was giddy, heady stuff, and her hands slipped lower, to his belt buckle and beyond, wanting to watch the look in his eyes turn from a smouldering grey ember into a leaping flame.

He groaned out her name as she pressed her palm against the hard straining heat she found there, and her fingers caressed him unrelentingly.

Impatiently, he undid his belt and yanked off his jeans, and suddenly he was nudging her knees wider aside, rising his body up and over hers, his face level with hers now, their breaths meeting and mingling as they panted their mutual desire.

'Payne!' She wanted to warn him that she was new at this, and probably wouldn't be very good, but he shushed her, pushing the hair from her damp forehead, his eyes as gentle as the softest mist.

'I'll be gentle,' he promised her.

And he was.

From the moment he entered her, Charmaine became lost in the sensation of him, deep inside, hot and powerful yet tender. She gasped and shuddered as her body rocked to the rhythm of his, accepting him, urging him on to greater, deeper thrusts, needing and wanting more, always more.

This time the tight, hard feeling was far more intense than before, so much so that she thought it would drive her out of her mind.

She was dimly aware that she was clinging to him, her fingernails scoring long angry red lines down his back. His face was taut with emotion and passion, and when he called out her name and shuddered atop her, she felt an answering climax wrack her own frame and suddenly she was soaring.

She soared for a long, long time, only slowly coming back down to earth.

Eventually she became aware of herself and her world again. The desk began to feel hard beneath her, his weight a warm, comforting crush that she never wanted to have removed.

Finally though, he pushed himself up, and looked wonderingly down at her, taking his weight on his straightening elbows and smiling the most heart-stopping smile she knew she would ever live to see.

His hair was dark and damp, his skin flushed with sweat. His eyes looked as deep as the ocean.

'I love you,' he said softly. 'I've never said that to any woman, Charmaine, I promise you. I've never loved any other woman, and I never will. Trust me.'

And Charmaine felt her heart sing with pure happiness. 'I believe you,' she said, and did.

It was true. A woman just knew.

'And I'll never let you down. You will always be able to trust me,' he urged.

And she understood exactly what he was saying. No more insane gambles. No more . . .

Suddenly she felt a cold hand clutch at her heart as an awful, overwhelming realisation suddenly hit her.

Yes, she could trust him.

But, once she'd told him about why she'd come to the island, and how cruelly she'd set out to deceive him, how brutally she'd intended to treat him . . .

How would he ever be able to trust her again?

CHAPTER THIRTEEN

Charmaine brushed back the tears from her face as she folded away her last pair of shorts and zipped up her suitcase.

'Hi, all set?' Lucy walked in and grimaced. 'Only the one case? You know for someone who designs such fab clothes, you sure travel light.'

Charmaine managed a laugh. 'You should see the Jonniee cases, though. They could take up the whole hold of a jumbo jet all by themselves.'

'I believe you. So any ideas yet on your wedding gown?' her sister asked brightly, and Charmaine stiffened.

'Oh, one or two,' she said, deliberately vague. 'And you — have you made up your mind what you want yet?'

'I don't know, sis, I'm sort of hovering between classic ivory, perhaps a short dress and a near invisible veil — or going really over the top with something in tartan,' Lucy laughed gaily.

Charmaine grinned. 'If you want over the top get Jo-Jo to do your wedding dress. He'll do you proud. If you want more traditional, just let me know.'

She'd offered to design her sister's wedding dress the moment Lucy had told her that Max was flying to England to meet their father, and that a spring wedding would follow as soon as his divorce was final.

She was also, ostensibly, supposed to be working on her own dress, but although Charmaine could picture it perfectly in her mind's eye, she had no intention of putting pencil to paper and bringing it into reality.

After all, she'd never wear it, so why torture herself?

'Right, I'd best get going. We don't want to miss the flight,' she said firmly.

'Sure you don't want me to come and see you off?' Lucy pressed, but Charmaine was already shaking her head.

'No, that's fine. I'm going with the rest of the gang. We came together, so it's nice to leave together as well.'

'Hmm, but unlike the fulminating Jinx and the rest of the crew, you'll be coming back,' Lucy sighed blissfully. 'It must be absolutely eating that red-headed witch's heart out that you got your man. And such a man.'

Charmaine grimaced. 'Oh, let's not gloat.' Especially, she thought sadly, since there's nothing to gloat about.

As far as the rest of the island and the media was concerned, she was flying home to get her affairs in order, collect her pet, and start on her trousseau, before returning to the island for the wedding of the century in the autumn.

Only Charmaine knew that she would never be coming back.

She hoisted her case onto the floor, trying to ignore the fact that her heart was breaking, and looked around her room in farewell. She'd been happy here — if only briefly.

'Next time you'll be staying at the Palace,' Lucy said, mistaking her look and the reason for it. 'Not this place. The main suite is fantastic. I haven't seen it,' she hastened to add, 'but I've heard rumours. Or are you and Payne thinking of buying a house now you're going to be an old married couple? After all, a casino isn't exactly the ideal place to raise kids is it?'

Charmaine bit her lip. She had no idea what Payne had in mind. And it didn't matter now, did it?

'Oh, we'll see,' she said vaguely, unable to take much more of Lucy's cheerfulness while her whole world was about to come to an end. Of course, she could stay, but then she'd have to tell Payne the truth, only to watch all that love and trust in his eyes dwindle to something hard and bitter.

No, it was far better this way.

Lucy watched her, a worried frown creasing her forehead. 'Not having second thoughts are you?' she half-teased, half-probed. 'About Payne, I mean.'

'Oh no,' Charmaine said truthfully. 'Payne's the love of my life, no doubt about it.' And her life with him would never have been dull. But that was all over now. It had been over the moment she realised that Payne, once he knew the truth about her, would never want to marry her in a million years.

Lying in his arms, her whole body still throbbing after the intense pleasure of their love-making, she had suddenly realised that that was her last moment of bliss.

Other women might be able to marry a man and keep quiet about it, hiding such a secret without a qualm. But she knew herself well enough to know that she was not one of them. Besides which, she'd be cheating him, and for someone with his mindset, that would be the ultimate sin. He was a gambler, fair and square. Marrying him without telling him who and what she really was, was the action of the dirtiest cheater ever to cross his path.

If he found out about it after they were married, he'd hate her, and she simply couldn't bear that. No, far better to get the pain over and done with now, and leave him free to find someone else.

Once she was safely back in England, she'd write him a long letter to explain everything, and return his ring. He wouldn't ever have to see her again, something he'd be bound to be grateful for. And she would have spared herself the heartache of seeing his love and trust turn to indifference.

A bellboy took her case to the taxi, one of several that was waiting, containing Jo-Jo and the rest of the gang.

She got into a taxi with Phil and Dee-Dee, who were looking at her with far more respect than ever before. Not only had she snared a wealthy and powerful husband for herself, but news had also spread about her real position at Jonniee. And suddenly she was no longer merely an awkward amateur model, but a woman of real power.

Even Jinx was forcing herself to be polite to her!

And it was a nice feeling to have Phil and Dee-Dee treat her like one of the bosses at last. She couldn't think why she hadn't 'come out' before!

She glanced out of the window as the taxi pulled away, taking a long, last, lingering glimpse of the Palace. She knew that Payne had an urgent and important meeting that morning for he'd told her so, which was why he wasn't able to take her to the airport himself, and she still blushed as she remembered the hard, deep, molten kiss he'd given her last night.

'Hurry back,' he'd husked, his eyes devouring hers as he'd lifted her fingers to his lips and kissed each fingertip in turn. 'I can't bear to have you out of my sight for too long.'

If only he knew the real truth, Charmaine thought now, with a lurch of pain so physical it almost brought her out of her seat, he'd never want to set eyes on me again.

She had no illusions on the score. For a man like Payne, a man who was used to doing all the running, a predator, a gambler, a man so sure of his masculinity and his place in the world's pecking order, to find out that he'd been duped by a woman would be a massive and irreparable blow to his pride.

And one that a brand-new love like theirs would never be able to withstand.

But oh . . . how she wished this wasn't happening! How she wished she could stay and marry him and live happily ever after.

She gripped her fingers together hard, not wanting the others to see her grief, and stared out of the window as Nassau International Airport came into view.

At the check-in desk, Jo-Jo sorted things out while she and the rest of the gang went into the cafeteria. Not that she was hungry. She ordered coffee and sat nursing it, only looking up when Jo-Jo finally joined her.

'There's been a bit of a mix-up, it appears,' he said, sliding out a chair and collapsing into it. 'Airlines! Don't you just love 'em? Apparently, you're not booked on this flight at all, and as it's full, you'll have to wait for the next one.'

Charmaine sighed wearily. 'Great.' Just what she needed.

Jo-Jo shrugged. 'Well, that's the way it is. I can't swap with you myself, because I need to get back in time for that meeting about the fashion outlet. And neither Phil nor his assistants will let the cameras and film go without them babysitting them every inch of the way. And you know the girls. They've all got things to do and places to go.'

Charmaine nodded listlessly. 'It's fine. I'll wait.' If she'd been less depressed and more alert, she might have picked up on the fact that her partner was talking too much, and looked far more excited than miffed about a genuine snafu.

As it was, she chatted with only half an ear until the boarding call, then followed him out into the main area and watched them go.

At the gate, Jo-Jo turned and waved frantically, a broad grin on his face.

Only then did Charmaine get a funny feeling running down her spine. A feeling of having been set up.

'So they've gone then,' a voice, a wonderfully familiar voice, said right behind her. 'Not that I have anything against them, mind, but I'm glad to have you on your own at last.'

Charmaine turned a pale, wide-eyed face to look up at him, and swallowed hard. 'I thought you had a meeting?'

Payne grinned. 'I lied.'

'B-but, what are you doing here?'

'Oh, a little birdie told me you wouldn't be leaving today.'

Charmaine closed her eyes briefly, then gave a weary smile. 'You set this up with Jo-Jo.'

'I told him I couldn't live with you, even for a day, and he agreed to help out.'

Charmaine sighed heavily. 'So am I really going to have to go and book my own flight out?'

Payne's smile faded.

'When were you going to tell me?' he asked softly, and her heart began to thump hard and loud. The room swayed a bit, then settled.

'Tell you what?' she whispered.

'That you weren't going to come back. You weren't planning on it, were you?' he added, when she simply stared mutely back at him.

At last she let out a long, slow breath. 'No. No I wasn't,' she admitted.

He nodded, but surprisingly didn't look very angry. Instead he slipped his hand around her arm and led her out of the airport. His sports car was illegally parked (naturally!) and she let him settle her inside with a dull feeling of resignation. When he roared away from the airport and drove them to a tiny, deserted, crescent-shaped beach, she tried not to think about the agony that lay ahead.

She should have known she could never fool a man like Payne. He'd probably seen right through her like glass. So it was going to be a head-to-head confession after all, and all the pain and angst she'd tried to spare them was now ahead of them.

Her heart ached as he wordlessly took her hand and led her onto the sand. Pink shells littered the beach, and out in the bay, a cheerful red, green, blue and yellow windsurfer's sail bobbed up and down on the waves. A tiny crab scuttled for cover, but apart from themselves, it was the only thing moving on the beach.

He sank down onto the white sand and patted the patch next to him. 'Come on. I won't bite.'

Not now, Charmaine thought. But just you wait. The irreverent thought actually made her smile.

Payne watched her as she sank next to him, and resisted the urge to reach out and kiss her. To lay her down against the sand and ravish her.

Ever since he'd taken her virginity, he couldn't wait to teach her more and more. He had a king-sized four-poster bed back at the Palace just waiting for them in his master suite; he wanted to introduce her to it and not let her out for the next year.

Or ten years.

Or the rest of their lives. But first they had to get things sorted.

'All right, first of all, let me apologise,' he said, making her nearly faint. She snapped her head around so fast, she went dizzy.

'You apologise? What on earth for? You haven't done anything wrong.' He'd been the only innocent one in all this sorry mess.

'For the way I made you accept my proposal at the casino. It was unfair, but in my defence, I wanted to make you see that we were meant to be together.'

Charmaine felt tears fill her eyes and quickly blinked them back. 'You knew you were going to win that bet, didn't you?' she said, with something approaching awe in her voice. 'I mean, there was never even the slightest doubt in your mind that if I'd said red, it would be black, or if I'd said black, then it would be red?'

Across the space of the few inches separating them, Payne smiled softly. 'No, sweetheart, I didn't have the faintest doubt. I knew that it was meant to be.'

Charmaine swallowed back a hard lump in her throat.

'I also knew it was going to be my last gamble,' he said, making her eyes widen even further.

'But why?' she'd breathed. Gambling was like meat and drink to him.

'Because, after that, there would never be anything worth gambling for again,' he said simply. Then he smiled. 'Besides, after we're married, I wouldn't want our kids to get into bad habits.'

She gulped. Tears blurred her vision, and she looked away. 'Payne, I can't marry you,' she choked.

'Why? Because you tried to con me?' Payne said offhandedly. 'Because you thought I'd done the dirty on your sister and you wanted to teach me a lesson? Forget it. I already have.'

Charmaine nearly fainted. 'Wh-what did you say?'

Payne smiled wolfishly. 'I'd already guessed why you'd come to the island. I thought it was rather sweet, actually, the way you charged to Lucy's defence. The maiden rushing to the desert island to slay the dragon. A bit of a twist on the old fairy story, but I liked it.'

'Payne, this isn't funny!' she cried. 'Don't you see? I was out for revenge. I would have had it too, if things hadn't turned out the way they did. So . . . so you see how impossible it is,' she said at last. 'I knew after we'd made love,' she blushed as she said this, 'that I couldn't marry you, not without telling you about everything. And I knew once I did that, you'd be furious and want nothing more to do with me. I thought I could spare us all this by flying to England and then . . . just not coming back.'

Payne waited until her voice had trailed away, then sighed. 'Charmaine, do I look furious?' he asked at last, and watched, his breath lodged somewhere in his throat, as she slowly turned towards him.

Her eyes looked full of bewilderment and hope. He thought it was quite possible that he'd never love her more than he did in that moment.

'N-no,' she said at last, still a little uncertainly.

'That's because I'm not. Oh, I grant you, at first I wasn't best pleased. And yes, maybe my ego took a bit of a battering. But it didn't take me long to find out that this thing between us was far stronger than my hurt pride. But far more importantly, what I really needed to know was — had you fallen for me as hard as I'd fallen for you? And there was only one way to find out. And that was to propose.'

Charmaine blinked. 'But how was that going to tell you anything?'

'Simple. If you jumped at the chance, then it meant you were still working to your plan. It would have suited you perfectly to publicly dump me at the altar, right?'

'Well, I wasn't going to go that far,' she demurred.

'But you didn't jump at the chance. Instead you looked shell-shocked. So you were obviously having second thoughts about me. Then I began to make love to you, just to be sure,' he carried on modestly, making her glance at him sharply.

'Oh you did, did you?' she huffed. 'And did I pass that test too?'

'Oh yes. With flying colours,' he said infuriatingly. 'So then I knew you loved and wanted me, but until we had all this Lucy stuff sorted out, we were stuck. So here we are,' he finished with a flourish, waving a hand around the deserted beach.

Charmaine gasped. 'You . . . you . . . you . . .'

'Clever thing?' he supplied innocently.

Charmaine huffed. 'That wasn't quite what I was going to say,' she said, then squealed as he suddenly lunged over her, rolling her onto the sand and looming over her.

'It worked though, didn't it?' he said smugly.

'Then you forgive me for what I planned to do,' she said, even now hardly daring to believe it.

'Forgive you with knobs on,' he said. 'Besides, I found it thrilling. I find you thrilling. And more than that,' he said, his voice suddenly serious, 'I love you. And want you. And you will marry me, or else.' He spoke almost harshly, and yet there was still an edge of pleading in his voice, a hint of vulnerability that touched her at the core.

Charmaine nodded. 'Of course I will marry you,' she husked, reaching out to touch his face tenderly. Then she grinned impishly. 'After all, I can hardly renege on a bet, now, can I?' she asked.

And kissed him.

Hard.

THE END

154

ALSO BY FAITH MARTIN

DI HILLARY GREENE SERIES
Book 1: MURDER ON THE OXFORD CANAL
Book 2: MURDER AT THE UNIVERSITY
Book 3: MURDER OF THE BRIDE
Book 4: MURDER IN THE VILLAGE
Book 5: MURDER IN THE FAMILY
Book 6: MURDER AT HOME
Book 7: MURDER IN THE MEADOW
Book 8: MURDER IN THE MANSION
Book 9: MURDER IN THE GARDEN
Book 10: MURDER BY FIRE
Book 11: MURDER AT WORK
Book 12: MURDER NEVER RETIRES
Book 13: MURDER OF A LOVER
Book 14: MURDER NEVER MISSES
Book 15: MURDER AT MIDNIGHT
Book 16: MURDER IN MIND
Book 17: HILLARY'S FINAL CASE
Book 18: HILLARY'S BACK
Book 19: MURDER NOW AND THEN

JENNY STARLING MYSTERIES
Book 1: THE BIRTHDAY MYSTERY
Book 2: THE WINTER MYSTERY
Book 3: THE RIVERBOAT MYSTERY
Book 4: THE CASTLE MYSTERY
Book 5: THE OXFORD MYSTERY
Book 6: THE TEATIME MYSTERY
Book 7: THE COUNTRY INN MYSTERY

MONICA NOBLE MYSTERIES
Book 1: THE VICARAGE MURDER
Book 2: THE FLOWER SHOW MURDER
Book 3: THE MANOR HOUSE MURDER

Thank you for reading this book.

If you enjoyed it please leave feedback on Amazon or Goodreads, and if there is anything we missed or you have a question about, then please get in touch. We appreciate you choosing our book.

Founded in 2014 in Shoreditch, London, we at Joffe Books pride ourselves on our history of innovative publishing. We were thrilled to be shortlisted for Independent Publisher of the Year at the British Book Awards.

www.joffebooks.com

We're very grateful to eagle-eyed readers who take the time to contact us. Please send any errors you find to corrections@joffebooks.com. We'll get them fixed ASAP.

Lightning Source UK Ltd.
Milton Keynes UK
UKHW042344210722
406135UK00014B/1010

9 781804 053966